My boxing talent is o all the boys, except Johnny Baker, like me. I'm not afraid to fight. I prove it my first day at the new school when I knock out Johnny's front tooth. I don't do it just to show off. I do it as a favor to my cousin Dottie Mae, who asks me to beat him up because he's making fun of her daddy, who has a wooden leg and is the school janitor. My uncle Harry has to drag his leg alongside and swing it forward as he sweeps the school's black pine floors with his wide broom. When my mom finds out what I've done, she guarantees me she'll find a way to knock the meanness out of me or she'll sure as hell die trying. I tell her I only hit Johnny once, and yes, I'm sorry, and yes, I'm ashamed. Then I have to agree that being sorry and ashamed won't bring back Johnny's front tooth, will it? And even though I say no, it won't, so far it hasn't stopped me from using my fists the way my daddy taught me.

HER
FATHER'S
DAUGHTER

Mollie Poupeney

For L.J.P.

Published by
Dell Laurel-Leaf
an imprint of
Random House Children's Books
a division of Random House, Inc.
1540 Broadway
New York, New York 10036

Visit us on the Web! www.randomhouse.com/teens

Educators and librarians, for a variety of teaching tools, visit us at
www.randomhouse.com/teachers

ISBN: 0-440-22879-4

RL: 5.3

Reprinted by arrangement with Delacorte Press

Printed in the United States of America

June 2002

10 9 8 7 6 5 4 3 2 1

OPM

CONTENTS

ACKNOWLEDGMENTS

I am grateful to the members of the Berkeley Tuesday writers' group. To Mary McLaughlin, Mary Tolman Kent, Mary Hanner, Dorothy Stroup, Sue Heath Brown, Alice Wirth Gray, Jane Strong, Ellen McKaskle, Naomi Cavalier, and Renata Polt, I say thank you with deep respect and affection for each one of you, and for the group we have sustained for more than twenty-five years.

To my teachers and advisors: Susan Griffin, Geoffrey Summerfield, Michael Rubin, Jeffrey Kline, Oakley Hall, Mary Webb, and the authors of every book I've ever read, including Big Little Books and the comic strips of the thirties and forties, a very strong and lasting influence—I say an overwhelming thank you for coming into my many lives.

To the thirty-some members of the Rossmoor Writers' Club of Walnut Creek, California, whose enthusiasm and encouragement spurred me onward and upward, I say thank you.

Special thanks go to my editor, Diana Capriotti, whose intelligence, quick wit, and enthusiastic dedication to my book—not to mention the kindly patience she has shown toward this author's peculiarities—have made it a rewarding experience for me. Also, the very precise and thorough copyediting of Jane Steltenpohl and Barbara Perris is very much appreciated.

Agnes Birnbaum, my agent loyal and true, is the one who made it all possible by embracing my work and knocking on those doors. Who could ask for more?

The Tale of the Frog

Daddy's fallen back to sleep and is snoring peacefully. The Sunday funnies cover his face and are spread on top of the blankets. Other sections of the paper rattle and wrinkle when Danny, straddling his soggy diaper, crawls on the bed and plops his soggy bottom on the pillow bunched in a ball beneath his daddy's head. "Funnies, Daddy, read me the funnies," he begs, and pulls the newspaper away from his daddy's face. He pokes a finger in one eye. "Wake up." Both eyes are squeezed tight. The lids wiggle and twitch. Danny giggles. Daddy isn't asleep, just playing pretend. Danny gouges harder to pry an eye open. As soon as he gets one open and is digging into the second, the first eye slams itself shut. Danny snickers so hard he doesn't hear his sister Maggie tiptoe into the bedroom until she throws herself with a thump and a crackle onto the bed and begins to tug on the other eyelid while Danny pinches a few eyelashes and gives Daddy's eyelid a hard ouchie pull.

"He's not asleep, he's just pretending," Maggie says. "You're just pretending, aren't you, Daddy?" she shouts into his ear. She gives the eyelid a hard upward tug and looks into a large brown eyeball surrounded by white, staring back at her.

Suddenly there is a thrilling growl. Daddy isn't going to take it anymore. With a ferocious roar and two large paws, he pounces. The two scramble to protect themselves and giggle even harder, for his strong claws have found their ribs, their stomachs, the bottoms of their feet. They scream with fear and joy.

Their older brother, Frankie, comes from the kitchen to lean against the doorjamb and watch. Maggie grabs Daddy's big toe and Danny leaps on Daddy's stomach.

"Oomph!" Daddy says. "Oh, so you think you're tough, do you? We'll just see about that now, won't we?" There's more squealing from Danny, more tickling from Daddy; then Daddy hollers real loud and jerks his leg, for Maggie has bit his big toe. Hard.

"That does it," Daddy says. "That's enough for now. Settle down, climb in, and if you're real good, I'll read you the funnies."

Which is exactly what Danny wanted in the first place. So Danny crawls under the covers on one side and Maggie on the other. Daddy raises his head off the pillow and says to Frankie, who is now watching from beside the window, "You, too, come on. Get in."

Frankie is wearing the blue-and-white-striped pajamas Santa Claus brought him. Mama says the blue matches the blue of his eyes. Frankie's skin is almost as white as the white stripes. "Too pale and skinny and too tall for his age," Mama says. "It's because he's growing way too fast."

But all Danny can feel when he looks at Frankie, standing by the window with the morning sun shining on his black hair, is how much he wishes he was as big as his big brother, who is learning how to be a real boxer. Frankie is lucky. He gets to take lessons from Daddy's old friend, Sailor Sharky, who owns the gym uptown above Brennan's meat market. They go there every Sunday afternoon, him and Daddy. They go alone. Not even Maggie gets to go watch Frankie put on the boxing gloves and get into the ring. Not even Mama, who wouldn't go for a million dollars, not even if you asked her on bended knees, she said.

"It's cruel to teach little boys how to beat up on each other so a bunch of grown men can sit around drinking and betting money on who's going to knock the other one down, or out—which is even worse! And don't you tell me it doesn't happen. I think it's barbaric," she said.

Which is when Daddy said to Mama, "Not another word. We're not raising us a pansy here. It's a man's world, and he's got to learn how to take care of himself, how to be a real man. And, by God, it's my job to teach him. This is the way my own daddy taught me, and I didn't turn out too bad, did I?" Daddy smiled at Mama. "When I was in the ring, you used to think I was pretty slick yourself—or have you forgotten?"

Mama turned and reached for the frying pan.

Daddy said, "I'm telling you, do it your way and you'd make a sissy out of him."

Mama just shook her head.

"Besides, the boys can't hurt each other with those big gloves. They might as well be hitting each other with goose-down pillows, right, son?" And Frankie mumbled something Daddy didn't hear and got a small flick on the side of his head with Daddy's thick fingernail to get his attention. "Did you hear what I said?"

"Yessir."

"You like it, don't you, learning from Sailor Sharky?"

"Yessir."

"Well, c'mon then. Let's show your mother how it's done." Daddy bent and hunched his left shoulder, burying his chin and bringing up his dukes, telling Frankie he could have the first punch. Maggie and Danny watched Frankie jab a couple of times. Daddy never made real fists or hit hard, but his hands were fast. It was more like he was slapping Frankie on his cheeks and the side of his head while he was telling him to keep his guard up, keep his guard up. They could see that Frankie was trying to do what Daddy was saying, but most of the time his eyes were half closed, fluttering, and he backed into the corner of the kitchen next to the stove.

He ended up crying. Mama was already crying and saying, "Delbert, stop, you hit him too hard! You're too rough. Quit now! You've been trying to get him to fight since he was in diapers—can't you see he does *not like* to fight?"

And Maggie said, "Frankie's just scared, Mama." Mama told her to mind her own business and to see if Danny didn't need his diaper changed. Which he usually did.

But Daddy gave Frankie a hard look and said, "No, Maggie's right. The boy has a yellow streak a yard wide right down the middle of his back. Don't worry— Sharky will cure him of that if anyone can."

Then he squatted down, face-to-face with Maggie, who was seven. "C'mon, Maggie, put up yer dukes. Let's show 'em how it's done." So Maggie cocked her fists and before Daddy had a chance to get his hands up, she whacked him so hard on the nose he landed on his rump. After he rubbed his nose to see if it was bleeding, he laughed, then looked mean and punched at Maggie as she circled and danced, jabbing first with her left, then her right, with her chin tucked in just like Daddy kept telling Frankie to do. Finally, Daddy stopped and caught her in a bear hug, mussed up her Dutch bob with a Dutch rub and told Mama that here was his real boy, that Maggie was his real boy. Then Maggie looked at Frankie like she knew that Daddy liked her better and she didn't care if everybody saw her grinning away.

Danny tried to leap on his daddy's back, yelling, "No, she's not, Daddy! *Maggie's a girl, Daddy! I'm the real boy! I'm the real boy!*" Frankie stood in the corner watching the three of them wrestling on the linoleum floor until Mama told him to go wash his face, she would make him some hotcakes and sausages for breakfast. And, for God's sake, to stop scratching at those little water blisters on his hands, which Mama called his eczemas.

So Danny is happy this morning when Frankie says okay, he'll listen to Daddy read the funnies. Frankie pushes Maggie over and crawls in beside her. She kicks at Frankie for crowding her, but only once, for Daddy is saying, "Well, am I going to read *Andy Gump,* or not?"

"Jammer Kids, Daddy! Jammer Kids!" Danny begs.

Maggie says, "No, read *Little Orphan Annie.*"

"I can't read *Little Orphan Annie.*"

"Why not?"

"Because Little Orphan Annie has no eyeballs. Never trust a person who can't look you straight in the eye."

"Then read *Little Annie Rooney.* I like her better anyhow," she says, and helps him turn the pages.

"Read them all, Daddy, read us everybody." Danny is snuggled so close to his daddy's shoulder that Daddy can't turn the page. He heaves his body into a sitting position and gives Danny a cranky look. "How am I gonna read all these funnies without a cup of joe? And a fag? Somebody better go tell his mama we got us an emergency in here." His voice growls at Danny like a mean old dog, but Danny only laughs.

"Me! I'll go, I'll go—*Mama! Mama! Daddy wants his joe and fags!*" He's hollering into his daddy's ear before he's shoved onto the floor and runs into the kitchen.

Mama says for Maggie to come get them, she's too busy cleaning the oven and too tired to wait on anybody. Her voice isn't loud, for she's right there in the kitchen on the other side of the wall.

After Daddy has slurped the coffee spilled into the saucer and finished off the cup and smoked his Camel cigarette, Maggie gives the ashtray to Frankie to put on the floor and says, "Okay, now read." The three of them are half-sitting, propped against the headboard, crowded in close, listening, trying to see every picture as Daddy reads.

"You sound just like him," Maggie says, and tries to copy the way Daddy mimics the Captain's accent, and then the high voices of those naughty Katzenjammer Kids, who always end up getting spanked "Chust in case."

Danny snuggles even closer. He's glad he doesn't have a daddy like the old Captain. Even with those stinks from beer and whiskey and cigarettes, his daddy is better than that mean old Captain. Danny's daddy always has a *reason* to spank, and it's always for someone's own good.

Last night, after eating two big bowls of white bean soup and ham hock for supper, his daddy'd said he had to go see a man about a horse, and Mama'd said, "Uh-huh. And by any chance, does that horse have a neon beer sign sitting on its saddle?" And when he had left for the Anchor Inn down on the waterfront, she had called after him to tell his friend Shorty Lumijarvi hello.

Barney Google and Popeye and Olive Oyl and Dick Tracy and Little Annie Rooney all seem to be tucked into bed with them. When Daddy quits reading, Maggie and Danny groan and twist, wanting more, and although Frankie is silent, he looks disappointed too. So Daddy says, "Well, okay, I'll do my most famous magic trick."

Maggie says, "I don't like your tricks. I already know all your tricks and they're not funny." One Saturday night when Mama and Daddy had company, Daddy took Maggie, who was five, to the corner of the living room, pointed to a pile of icky brown poop, and asked her, Did she do that mess? Shame on her. Then when she was saying no no and crying her eyes out, he picked up the icky thing in his bare fingers and showed her it was just a joke, a trick made out of colored plaster. And then he laughed and tried to hug her in his arms. Everyone else laughed too. But Maggie didn't laugh. And she wouldn't let Daddy hug her.

Now Daddy says, "No, you don't."

"Yes, I do, I'll show you." Maggie shows how she can pull off her own thumb. Danny tries to do it too and can't, and Frankie snorts and shakes his head. "See?" Maggie says. "Just like I said. Your tricks are dumb."

"Well, okay, then. I'll tell you a story. Danny, did you ever hear 'The Tale of the Frog'?"

Danny takes his thumb out of his mouth. "Huh-uh."

"You, Maggie?"

"Is this the song about the frog who went a-courtin' uh-hum, uh-hum?"

"No, this is 'The Tale of the Frog.' Didn't I ever tell you?" He looks at Frankie.

Three heads are shaking no.

"Okay then, here goes—*ahem!*—'*The Tale of the Frog.*'" Daddy pauses, then sucks in a deep breath and lets it out slowly. "*He hasn't any.* There! Now hand me my ashtray, Frankie. I think I'll have another smoke."

Three pairs of eyes stare at him.

"That's not a story," Maggie says.

"Did I say it was a story?"

"You said it was a story about a frog's tail."

"Did you ever see a tail on a frog?" Daddy asks.

"No."

"Well, there you are. Like I said—he hasn't any. And that's all she wrote." Daddy gives them a satisfied smile. "Well, Danny, how did you like my story?"

Danny sticks out his lower lip. "What story? I didn't hear no story. What happened to the frog?"

Maggie interrupts. "That's cheating." She gives Daddy her hardest shove.

"No, Maggie, that's storytelling."

"Well, then, what's the difference between telling a story and telling a lie?"

Daddy's eyebrows suddenly jump up on his forehead, and his face screws up funny. He says real quick, "Oops! Stick your heads under the covers, kids, I'm gonna spit in the air!"

They look at him, startled, then duck their heads under the covers just as the gasses from last night's bean soup escape and rattle around in those dark spaces, booming and bouncing beneath the heavy wool blankets.

Three heads pop out into daylight. Three mouths suck air.

Danny's eyes are wide. "You let a stink. You said that wasn't nice to let a stink around other people, Daddy."

Maggie gives him a dirty look. "You did that on purpose. You tricked us. That's not fair."

"Well, honey, you got to learn sometime that life's not always fair. Isn't that right, Frankie? Hey! Frankie! You come right back here! Where are you going? Hey, stick around—we're going to the gym this afternoon. *You've got your lesson with Sharky—I said come here! You don't walk out on me!*"

Daddy crosses his arms. He's waiting. He's scowling. Maggie is very quiet and pretends to be reading the funnies. Danny can tell that this time his daddy isn't playing pretend. But Frankie doesn't return to the bedroom.

Daddy says, "Damn that Mama's boy! Danny, get out of my way. Maggie, hand me my pants. It looks like I'm just going to have to teach that young man a lesson he'll never forget." Daddy stands in his long johns and pulls on his pants.

He doesn't hear Maggie ask again, her voice quieter, "What's the difference between telling a story and telling a lie?" Because Daddy is already in the kitchen hollering at Frankie. Maggie looks over at her younger brother.

Danny yawns. He sticks his thumb in his mouth and puts his head on Daddy's pillow. He closes his eyes. He doesn't know and he doesn't care.

But Maggie does.

Goofy John

I hear my daddy tell my mama to damn well keep his little girl Maggie—that's me—away from that queer Goofy John because he's not only six shingles short of a shed roof, he's a pervert.

Mama says Daddy shouldn't say such things about the poor man, a disabled veteran like that, whose lungs had been gassed up with mustard in the Great War. She's sure he wouldn't harm a fly.

So Daddy cusses a few bad words and says, "My God, woman! Don't you understand what I'm saying? Don't you know what he is?"

And she says, of course she knows, everyone knows he's some kind of artist who makes those little seashell dolls he sells to the tourists who come to Nye Beach, and Fern says he also used to be an officer in the army, which is why he dresses like that, and yes, John is a little peculiar, you know, eccentric. He's a loner. Like she said, he's an artist, and aren't artists always a bit different? she says. But mainly, she says, he's suffering from that terrible lung trouble.

Daddy's laugh doesn't sound friendly when he says, Oh, no, she has it all wrong, and he—Goofy—doesn't have him, my daddy, fooled for a minute. He's just a goddam pansy, that's all there is to it!

And Mama says she wonders, could Daddy by any chance be just a little bit jealous because he was too young to be a doughboy in the war and didn't get to have the great adventure of fighting in France for his country like Goofy did?

This makes Daddy cuss a lot more, so he stomps out of the house and slams the back door. Which is what he does sometimes.

Since no one says anything to me, I pretend I don't hear anything. That way, I can keep on visiting Goofy in his shop down on the boardwalk. It doesn't matter to me that I'm only seven-going-on-eight and Goofy's older'n my daddy. Goofy John is my good friend. Here's why.

It's because he likes me.

Also because he makes those little dolls. He lets me watch him and sometimes help him paint their little eyes with the big black dots with the white showing all around—well, so far only once. And I also collect the

littlest blue mussel shells for him from under the Natatorium. He uses them for the feet of every one of his
dolls. I never ask, but sometimes he gives me a doll to
keep for my very own. I have four Goofy dolls. I keep
them in my secret treasure box under my bed. I wrap it
up with adhesive tape, but my little brother, Danny,
gets into it anyway.

I sneak out of the house early this morning so I don't
have to take Danny along. I just want to see if Goofy's
come back from the beach. I like to see all his treasures—he finds all kinds of good stuff. Periwinkles.
Limpets. Broken bits of abalone. Pieces of razorback
clamshell—and different kinds of lacy sea moss or fern.

We live right above the boardwalk, so I can slide
down the sandstone bank, using my feet as brakes, and
land on the sandy road that goes down to the beach.
The road is there so people who own cars can drive
down and have picnics on the beach, swim in the warm
pool in the Natatorium or outside in the freezing ocean,
or just drive along the water's edge where the sand is
hard. Usually people are drinking beer and singing and
whooping like cowboys. Sometimes the people are having such a good time they forget the car and it gets
caught when the tide sneaks in too fast. Then they just
have to wait for the tide to turn around and go back out
again. Sometimes, even if the salt water don't wreck the

engine, the cars have to be towed out. Mama and Daddy laugh when they see this happening. We don't have that kind of trouble. We don't own no car.

Goofy's shop is the first one at the top of the boardwalk. When I cross the road, I can see before I knock on the door that Goofy isn't in there. The lights are out. I try the door. It's locked. I knock anyway, hoping Goofy is in the back room where he lives and does his work. When he doesn't show, I press my nose to the glass, looking inside at all the little Goofy dolls lined up on the windowsill and on a table next to the window. They are standing around the big green and blue balls of handblown glass that have washed up on our beach. Goofy says they're fishing floats, coming all the way across the ocean from Japan.

Right away I spot the doll with the biggest eyes. This is the one Goofy let me paint the other day. I can hardly see where I smeared the paint and had to wipe it off with a wet rag so I could paint in the eyes again. Goofy told me, "You're a very apt pupil, Maggie, you are learning." I don't know what "apt" means, but I know from the way his eyes squint up that it's something good and that makes me feel good. Goofy is a real artist. I don't tell him that's what I want to be when I grow up. But I do—I want to be a real artist. I hope I don't forget.

On the man dolls the heads are shiny shells with big black eyes with the whites showing. On the lady dolls Goofy paints black curling eyelashes just like Betty Boop's. The men carry slim driftwood canes, and the ladies, they carry little umbrellas made of a lacy seaweed fern or moss, dried and stiff and fancy. Sometimes the color is purplish, sometimes a light tan. Goofy fills the shoes—my mussels—with white plaster from Paris in France to hold the furry white pipe cleaner legs in place.

On the men's shoes he paints white spats. On the ladies' he glues tiny wooden heels, painted pink. Once in a while he has a lady and a man holding hands and walking or dancing or sitting on a little driftwood bench looking into each other's big black-and-white eyes. Sometimes when I look at them, they begin to look just like Goofy himself, who's very skinny and tall, except Goofy has tiny light blue eyes, long black hair, and wears those old glasses with wire frames.

When it's cold and rainy and real windy on the beach, Goofy wears a wool knit cap underneath his rusty old helmet. He always wears those horse-riding pants and old leather things he calls puttees buckled below his knees, but the bottom buckles are missing so they hang over his black high-top tennis shoes and bounce on his shins when he walks. His shoes are always a little wet from walking on the beach. Sometimes he forgets he's already done his collecting and goes out again when it's dark, thinking it's real early in the morning. Mama says it's the mustard that makes him forgetful.

I feel good that Goofy needs my help. I decide to collect the little mussel shells while I'm waiting for him to come back from the beach, but first I stop at Mrs. Turner's Salt Water Taffy and Candy Store. The smell of sweet chocolate floats in the air and makes my stomach beg for a chocolate-covered cherry.

Heading down the boardwalk, I'm sniffing the air like a dog. Near Mrs. Turner's door I spot something brown and round and shiny lying on the sidewalk. Oh, boy! Someone dropped a chocolate-covered cherry! I look through the window to see if Mrs. Turner is watching, but she's busy at the taffy-pull machine. Good! I stoop down and grab the shiny brown ball and bring it up to my mouth. Just in time I get a whiff, make a face, shout "Ick!" and throw the stinking doggy-do as far as I can. I scrub my hand on my back pocket, mad at the whole world and especially at ugly old Raynaldo, Mrs. Turner's Chihuahua.

Just then here comes Raynaldo waddling out of the alley next to the store. He strolls over, lifts his hind leg and leaves a yellow puddle as big as a penny next to my left foot. I stomp into the candy store, Raynaldo at my heels. Mrs. Turner looks up from behind the taffy machine.

"Your dog pooped in front of your door," I say.

"He shouldna did that."

"I almost ate it."

"You shouldna did that, neither."

"I thought it was a chocolate-covered cherry."

"I don't feed Raynaldo chocolate-covered cherries. He don't like them."

"Well, I do," I say, looking into the glass case, which holds hunks of honeycomb and chocolate bark and chocolate creams and the chocolate-covered cherries.

Mrs. Turner leans over the counter with a rag to wipe the glass in front of my face. "Well, he don't. So if you're not gonna buy nothing, just run along. I don't have all day. And quit breathing on the glass."

I take a step back.

Raynaldo comes to stand by my foot again. The nails on his two back feet are making tapping sounds on the linoleum floor. I turn around to face him. His black marble eyes have a sneaky look.

Mrs. Turner says, "And leave Raynaldo alone. He's got bladder trouble."

"Bladder trouble? What's that?"

"You'll find out someday." Mrs. Turner pets the

silky rope of pink taffy like it's a sleeping kitty. I watch her. The flavor is strawberry, another one of my very favorites.

So I don't see Raynaldo when he lunges and grabs me by my left shin with his two front paws. His hindquarters begin to make strange pumping jabs against my foot. His sharp toenails dig into my leg. "Quit it!" I holler, and shove at his head, but he's sticking to my leg like snot. I swing it full circle and then some, but Raynaldo, he's stuck and panting hard. His hind end just won't quit, it just keeps hammering away. His black eyes bulge and he's staring into my face like he don't see me.

"Make him quit!" I holler again.

Mrs. Turner leans over the counter and peers at old Raynaldo. "Well, quit playing with him then."

"I'm not, I'm not! He's gone crazy! What's the matter with him? Is he having himself a bladder attack?"

Mrs. Turner sighs and shakes her head. "Oh, quit your hollering, he won't last long. He can't keep it up. He's old." She turns away and is scraping chips of dark chocolate off a metal tray into a bowl. Pretty soon Raynaldo slows down. He unwinds his hold and sprawls, still panting. His tongue lays on the gray linoleum looking just like a tiny slice of baloney. His ears twitch. I move two steps back, ready to kick again, but

Raynaldo's eyes droop and close. He's asleep, but I still don't trust him.

I stay there near the counter watching the last splinters of chocolate fall into the bowl. Mrs. Turner finishes wiping the counter and looks at me, her hands on her hips.

"So? You want something, or don'tcha?"

"How much are they today?"

"How much is what today?"

"The chocolate-covered cherries."

Mrs. Turner snorts and shoves her gold-rimmed glasses higher on her nose. "The same as yesterday and the day before. You got a penny, or don't you?"

I shake my head.

"I didn't think so." Mrs. Turner shuffles into the back room and comes back with a bowl of water, which she places on the floor next to Raynaldo's head. I wait for Mrs. Turner to say something else, but she doesn't even look at me.

Finally I say, "But I'll get me one."

"I won't hold my breath," she says.

With my hand on the doorknob, I turn and ask, "Did you see Goofy today?"

"He goes down before it's light, so how would I see him?"

I shrug. "He's not in his shop."

"It ain't my business to keep track of every soul on this boardwalk. I mind my own business, and you should mind yours. Quit pestering that poor sick man and stop calling him that fool name. His Christian name is John. And quit pestering me! Now, get yourself back home where you belong! Scat!"

I give her a dirty look. I don't have to go home if I don't want to. And before I do, I'm going to get those mussel feet for Goofy.

So I go down the boardwalk past the shop that sells sailor hats and colored pennants with "Newport, Oregon" painted on them, and those cute little naked celluloid Kewpie dolls whose stomachs get dented real easy if you squeeze them just a teeny bit. The store is closed. No one ever comes here until afternoon when the wind might *maybe* stop blowing so hard and so cold, and the sun might *maybe* begin to break through the foggy sky.

When I get near the Natatorium, I spy the first flattened cigarette butt. I pick it up and squeeze it almost round and put it in the Ex-Lax box in my pocket, along with the matches I've sneaked.

I find more cigarette butts on the porch floor of the Natatorium, where people come at night to sit in the dark and listen to the crashing of the waves. I collect a Wings butt, a Domino butt, a Lucky Strike butt, and a Camel butt and put them in the Ex-Lax box.

Beneath the porch floor, which Goofy calls the portico, huge round black logs hold it up. Big rocks covered with slimy green moss are piled up to keep the bank underneath from getting washed away by the waves when the storms come in winter. I love the way this place stinks of salt and rotting seaweed. It's my secret hideout. I come here when I want to be by myself and watch the waves roll in and out, and to think, and to collect my mussel shells. And this here is where I come to smoke.

I flick my thumb across the head of the stick match the way my daddy does with his thick yellow thumbnail. But my thumbnail is all chewed up so it slips off the match head. I scratch it on a boulder. It breaks and falls into the green slimy moss. I strike a second match on the rivet of my overalls and suck on the short Camel butt. A flame shoots up close to my nose. I smell the familiar stink of burnt eyelashes and singed eyebrows. This happens almost every time I smoke. I swipe my hand across my face to make sure I'm not on fire. I suck in and blow out the smoke and, like always, I cough and cough. My head swirls. The breakers are fuzzy white and blurry. I lean against a piling while the waves come in and crash down on the beach. Finally my dizziness goes away and my eyes can see again. This happens every time too. I like it.

Pretty soon I find a small rock, and I pound away on the mussels stuck to the pilings and rocks. I fill my pocket—but not the one with the Ex-Lax box—and climb down to the beach. Maybe Goofy is coming this way with his gunnysack full of good stuff. I look toward the Coast Guard station, but I can't see past the bluff, the one Daddy calls Jump-off Joe's. It sticks out like a big thumb close to the ocean. I look the other way, toward the lighthouse. No Goofy. The wind is cold and blowing sand. It stings my face like icy needles. The sun is still hiding somewhere behind low clouds.

I hurry back up the boardwalk. I'll stop at Goofy's shop one more time, just to be sure. Maybe he passed me when I was hiding under the Natatorium and feeling funny from the smoke. When I pass the candy store, I pretend I don't see Mrs. Turner, but I see her anyway, waving me away with chocolate-covered fingers. Raynaldo is probably still asleep, drooling all over the floor. I don't care. He stinks.

The lights are on in Goofy's shop. The door is unlocked.

I call, "Goofy? You here?"

"Back here, Maggie."

I pass through the shop into the workroom. He's

sitting at his table. "Goofy, you're back. I didn't see you on the beach."

"I saw you," he says.

I feel my stomach drop. Goofy doesn't know I smoke. Did he see me under the boardwalk? "Where?"

"At Mrs. Turner's. You were busy, so I didn't stop."

"Mrs. Turner's a big stingy-gut."

When Goofy smiles he shows his long gray teeth. I see the wet gunnysack on his table, the same table he uses to make his dolls and the same table where he eats his food, except I've never seen Goofy eat. "Oh! Look! You got a lot of stuff. What'd you find?"

"See? A big chunk of abalone shell, might've come all the way from California. I'll break this up, make little French berets for the ladies. And here." He hands me a small white shell full of hard gray stuff.

"What is it?"

"An old clamshell. Might've been stirred up from the ocean floor by a typhoon or an earthquake and deposited on our shore."

"What's that gray stuff inside? It looks like sidewalk."

"You're right, it is a type of cement, Maggie. It's a petrified clamshell filled with Mother Nature's cement, see? Been in the ocean for a long, long time. A real discovery." He hands it to me. It feels heavy, like a rock.

"How long?"

"Maybe millions of years, maybe almost as old as the Earth. You want it?"

"Are you sure? Gee, thanks!" Another treasure for my secret treasure box. When I start to put it in my pocket, I remember the mussel shells. I pile them on the table. "I got you some more feet."

"Good. What do I owe you?"

He always asks me that, like it's a joke, and I always say "You don't owe me anything," because I'm hoping he's going to give me another doll, which, as I said, he's done four times before. I pause, then say, "Would it be all right? Could you maybe pay me a penny this time?"

Goofy's tiny eyes are a very light blue and so clear I can sometimes see right through them when he's standing sideways and the light is hitting his eyes just right. This doesn't happen very often because there's only that one lightbulb hanging on a fuzzy wire in the middle of his workroom, and he wears those old-fashion glasses with little specks of dandruff sticking to them like snow. He takes off his glasses and opens his eyes wide and leans real close to me. His breath smells like a sour dishrag.

"A penny?"

I nod my head and look at my feet. I feel ashamed that I've asked my friend for money. I look around the room. Goofy's dented tin cup and a tin dish sit on a shelf above the sink, and some seashells are drying on the small drainboard. On the plywood walls, hanging on nails, are his things from what he calls his Waterloo, those scratched and scraped leather things he calls puttees, that rusty helmet he wears on the beach over his wool knit hat, and a black mask with big bug eyes and a tin can for a nose, hanging by elastic straps. Goofy calls this mask his "nemesis." He likes to use words like "pacifist" and "vegetarian" and "icthy-something" and "anemone." Sometimes he asks me to repeat the words after him. He knows I'm collecting big words.

"Maggie? Did I hear you say one penny?"

"Uh-huh." I'm still looking at Goofy's walls. My cheeks are burning hot.

"Well, Maggie, yes, that sounds to me like an excellent bargain."

I look up and meet his eyes, even tinier now because he's smiling. "It does?"

"It certainly does," he says. He reaches into his pocket and feels around; then he takes my hand. In my palm he places two pennies and curls my fingers over them. "We have now negotiated a firm business agreement, a real bona fide contract." He smiles and holds out his hand and I hold out mine. We shake.

"Gee, thanks. Thanks a lot! I gotta go now."

He starts to laugh but ends up with one of those coughing spells. I try not to break anything running out of the shop on my way to the candy store.

Old Raynaldo is nowhere to be seen so I walk straight into Mrs. Turner's Salt Water Taffy and Candy Store. I'm squeezing my two pennies in my fist.

Mrs. Turner is wrapping pieces of strawberry taffy in little squares of wax paper. "Oh, no, two times in one day? I say no, no, no, no! You get on home. I'm too busy! Don't you got a mother who needs you?" She shakes her head and glares at me.

I stand right there where the chocolate-covered cherries are waiting behind the glass and don't budge. I say, "I want two chocolate-covered cherries," and I place my two pennies on top of the showcase.

Mrs. Turner squints at me over her glasses, picks up the pennies, and shakes her head. She reaches into the case and takes the shiny round ball on the very top of the mound and puts it in a little brown ruffled paper cup. Then, very slowly, she does it a second time. She steps over to the counter, puts the two chocolate-covered cherries down, and places my pennies in a tin box. Then she picks up the two candies in their fancy ruffled papers and hands them over the counter. I expect her to say "thank you," but she doesn't even smile. And here I am, a brand-new customer!

I smell the sweet, sweet flavor of chocolate and almost cram one into my mouth right there in front of Mrs. Turner. But I don't. I leave the store. I want to be alone when I take that first bite. At the door, I remember my manners and say, "Thank you, Mrs. Turner." She just grunts at me. But I don't care! I've got two chocolate-covered cherries in my hand!

I run to the alley between the candy store and Goofy's shop, my heart going bang-bang-bang and the delicious smell of those chocolate-covered cherries floating up into my nose.

First, I decide I will begin with very small bites. But all of a sudden, there goes the whole thing right in my mouth. One bite, and all this sweet cherry juice is squirting on my tongue and filling the back of my throat! I chew and suck and chew, blending cherry and chocolate and the sweet swirling taste of cherry juice. But I don't swallow, not yet. No, I just hold it all like a spongy ball, sucking until only a little bit is sticking to the roof of my mouth. Then I swallow and cram in the second one. This one I almost swallow whole. But I don't, for I want it to last forever. So again I take my time. Finally I suck on my tongue and my teeth for the very last taste of cherry, juice, and chocolate.

I start to run home. I wave at Goofy, who's re-arranging some of his dolls on the windowsill. He waves back and hurries to his door.

"Maggie, wait! I forgot to tell you something—did you go around the point at Jump-off Joe's today?"

"No, I just got you your feet, that's all." I don't tell him about the smoking, but I feel my face burn.

"Have you smelled anything funny up at your house?"

I start to say that both my brothers stink in different ways, and Daddy, when he's stopped off at the Anchor Inn on his way home from work. But Goofy looks so serious, I only say, "Like what?"

"Something peculiar, like you've never smelled before?"

"I don't think so. Why?" I'm beginning to get nervous. "Is it something real bad?"

"Well, I don't expect it's anything to get too bothered about, but there's a whale on the beach just below the bluff. It looks like it's been there for a while."

"A real whale? Just below Jump-off Joe's?"

Goofy nods. "A good-sized one too. A gray whale. It's a little early to be migrating. It was getting pretty ripe already earlier this morning."

"How'd it get there?"

"Looks like it beached itself. Whales do that when they're sick or confused. Nobody knows why. It's a mystery."

"You mean it's dead?"

"Oh, yes, indeed, it's dead, all right. You'll get a good whiff of it pretty soon, I'm afraid."

"I've never seen a real whale."

"I don't think you'll want to see this one, Maggie. The poor old fellow's been dead for a while. You better tell your mother to close all her windows, okay? And tell her I'm so very sorry about the whale. It's all my fault, you know."

"What do you mean? What did you do?" What could Goofy, who's always coughing, do to make a whale land on our beach, then rot away?

"Well, first of all, I haven't been going south to check the beach beyond Jump-off Joe's, so I didn't see it until today when I decided I should go down toward the Coast Guard station. Sometimes the tide is too high to get around when it is still too dark to see the shore-line. But I should have. Then I could have reported it to the Coast Guard a week or so ago . . . if I had, your family wouldn't be plagued with this disagreeable situation. Please tell your mother how much I regret my negligence." And just saying all this makes Goofy begin to cough his head off. Finally he stops, takes off his glasses, and wipes his eyes. I feel real bad to see him like this. And so will my mama when I tell her that Goofy is getting sick again.

Panting for air, he says, "Oh, and tell her again thanks for the lovely loaf of bread yesterday. It made a tasty dinner. She's always so kind." He waves his hand and goes inside. I hear him coughing again. These are the most words Goofy has ever said to me at one time before he starts his coughing spells, so maybe he's getting better. I can't wait to get home and tell Mama there's a whale on my beach! Oh, boy!

Mama isn't so happy when I tell her the news. "Oh, God—I don't want to hear this! A dead whale on the beach? Close the doors and all the windows, quick! I thought I smelled something strange, but I've been baking all morning, so I thought it was just the yeast in the starter. What a mess. Now, what are we going to do with a rotten whale?"

Danny wants to know if the whale can get us.

"No, dummy," Frankie, my big brother, says, looking out the kitchen window toward the boardwalk and scratching at those tiny blisters on his hands that Mama calls his eczema.

"It's not down there," I tell him. "It's the other way, just below Jump-off Joe's."

Danny wants to know if the whale jumped.

I tell him, like it's not so important, "No, it just got washed up on the sand by a huge wave and couldn't get back into the water, that's all." I don't want him following me and falling off the bluff when I go to discover the whale for myself. It could be dangerous for a little kid. Danny's not quite three. He always wants to follow me around.

Mama brushes some hair back from her forehead. Her face is red from having to keep the stove going so the oven can bake bread for us and Daddy's friends every day—and also a loaf for Goofy. She gives us baloney sandwiches for lunch and tells us to stay inside the house until Daddy gets home.

"And no fighting, you understand? I've got to bake this last batch, so get out of my kitchen, all of you."

I duck into the back bedroom and open the window Frankie has just closed. It's usually open because of the pee smell—Frankie's, not little Danny's. I crawl out and pull the window shut and run down the street past the house of Mama's friend Aunt Fern and past the empty old house on the corner I think is maybe haunted.

There is a low metal fence where the road bends and turns left, and behind the fence is the path that goes toward the bluff called Jump-off Joe's. Daddy says the fence is supposed to keep people from taking a long jump off a short pier, like Indian Joe did a long time ago, way before we moved here last year from the mountains above Tillamook. That's where we used to live when Daddy was still a logger, before the big fire burned down all the trees. We had to take a log train down from Saddle Mountain in the middle of the night to get away from the fire. I don't remember much about it.

I pass the fence all excited until I get closer to the edge of the bluff. When I look out over the ocean— even before I look down where the whale is supposed to be—my knees begin to wobble and shake. I feel dizzy, like I'm going to jump right off, like Indian Joe did, so I plop my rump down on the ground real quick and scoot myself back until I can breathe again, and my stomach quits trying to drop out of my body.

But instead, my stomach decides to bounce back up with a sick jerk, and there's this awful taste in my throat. Some real icky puke comes flying out of my mouth and lands in the grass in front of me. Little bits of red cherry and hunks of chocolate smeared in stringy pink spit and stuff. I know what it is. I mean, what it used to be. I look away and take another breath, and all of a sudden, the stink of the whale hits me and I'm throwing up again. And again.

I stagger home. Mama doesn't notice me until it's almost dinner time. "You're looking a little green around the gills," she says. "What's the matter? You getting sick?"

"I think it's the whale, Mama."

"Oh, I know, it's getting real bad. I'd like to know how anyone's going to sleep tonight. Are you hungry? Do you think you can eat something?" She feels my forehead.

"I don't think so."

Danny and Frankie are hanging around the kitchen sniffing and rubbing the tops of the warm loaves of bread, saying they're starving, and can't they have just one slice, please, please, please? Mama, who is peeling a potato, cuts it in half. "Here, you two, this will hold you until dinner." Then she gives me a funny look. "Maggie, we forgot John."

"I'll go right now."

Mama looks at the clock sitting on the shelf above the stove next to the green glass jar of bread starter she's kept alive since I was a baby. "I don't know. You'll have to hurry—your daddy should be home any minute—well, okay, but be quick." Then she hugs me and whispers, "And don't let your daddy see you."

"I won't." And out I go, sliding down the bank, hugging the warm loaf of bread wrapped in newspaper.

The light is on in Goofy's shop.

"Goofy? You here? I got you some new bread."

"Back here, Mag—" Then he's having another one of his coughing fits. He sounds like a barking seal.

What I see makes me stop at the doorway. Goofy is struggling to get himself out of his old army bed. He props himself up against the iron-pipe bed frame, wheezing and trying to get his breath.

"Goofy, what's the matter with you? You sick?"

His chest is pumping up and down. When it slows down a little, he sighs. "I'm okay, just that same old thing that comes and goes. Please tell your mother thanks for me, will you do that?"

"You always say that."

"I know. How's the whale? I mean, do you smell it at your house?"

"Can't you smell it? I can smell it right now. It smells worse than an outhouse. You sure you can't smell it? It's making me kind of sick." I don't mention what happened to me earlier at Jump-off Joe's.

"Not with this cold. You better not come back for a few days. I don't want to infect you with my germs."

"Does this mean you're not going down on the beach tomorrow?"

"Oh, well, I think I'll go. I've got to give the poor old fellow a decent burial."

"Burial? How do you do that?"

"Just shovel out a great big hole so he can slide right in, then cover him up." He's coughing again. He leans his elbows on his knees and rests his head in his hands. I can hardly hear him when he says, "You'd better go now, Maggie."

Goofy looks like he's too sick to go anywhere tomorrow. He waves me away, still coughing and spitting something into an old greenish gray hankie, the color my mama calls army color. I tiptoe out. Seeing Goofy sick like that scares me.

Back in the kitchen, I say, "Mama, Goofy's sick in bed. He coughs and coughs."

"Oh, honey, I know. It's those bad lungs. It's taking its toll. You better not bother him for a while. He needs his rest."

"He says he's going to bury the whale in the morning."

"Don't believe him. He's just saying that. He's not strong enough—oh, finally, there's your father." She puts her finger to her lips. "Remember, not a word."

At the front window, I watch Daddy's pal Shorty Lumijarvi park his old Model T pickup at the curb. Daddy gets out and heads for the house, and so does Shorty. Since the big Tillamook fire, they've worked together on the pile driver out in the middle of the bay, building a new jetty.

Daddy's carrying a brown paper bag. Mama sees the bag and says, "Not that again tonight." She drains the hot water from the potatoes into another pan and slams it on the drainboard. She'll save the potato water for Frankie to drink in the morning while he eats his Wheaties. Mama says he needs the extra nourishment because he's growing too fast, being only ten and tall as a thirteen-year-old. Every night she rubs mineral oil and Campho-Phenique on the stretch marks on his back and calamine lotion on his hands. What with all that stuff on Frankie's body and with Frankie having to wear those white flannel mittens so he won't scratch his eczema in his sleep, let alone trying not to wet the bed, my big brother Frankie is a real mess.

Mama tells us kids to eat right away, then get out of the kitchen. "Go outside and play."

"It stinks worser outside," Danny says.

"Oh! You're right! Well, hurry up and eat. You can play in the other room. I don't care. Just go somewhere else."

I say, "I'm not hungry." I give my plate to Frankie, who starts eating the food—doesn't even say thanks— and I run to say hello to Daddy, coming in the front door in his greasy black work clothes.

"Whew! What's that terrible stink out there?"

"It's the whale, Daddy! It's down on the beach rotting all over the place!"

He shifts the bag so he can grab me for a hug. I smell the beer on his breath. Shorty and Daddy head for the kitchen and I hear glasses clink and know it's going to be another one of those Saturday nights that ends up with Mama crying in the bedroom and Daddy singing and shouting in the kitchen. And me trying to stay asleep on the daybed in the living room.

After Shorty and Daddy finish off the jar of pickled pigs' feet and the four quarts of homemade beer they'd picked up from Dave the bootlegger, I hear Shorty ask, "How're you gonna get rid of a rotten whale in yer backyard, Smokey, huh? Bury it in the sand?"

I quit playing Chinese checkers with Frankie and go sit quietly on the other side of the kitchen doorway where I can peek and listen in without anybody seeing me. It sounds like Shorty has the same idea as Goofy.

"Bury a rotting hulk of blubber in the sand? How do you propose to do that, my good friend?"

"Well, just dig a big hole and push him in it, that's how."

"Who's going to be the one doing the pushing? And the digging? You? You'd have to dig that hole *under* the whale, you understand? So it can topple right in, and if it doesn't land right on top of you, you'd die of asphyxiation just from the smell even before you shovel out one load of sand. And do you realize how long and deep that hole would have to be? We're talking about many tons of whale blubber here. No, no, my friend, there's only one way." He tips a bottle into the glass, but the bottle's empty. So are the others. He looks at Mama, who's standing by the drainboard with her arms crossed.

"How's 'at?" Shorty asks.

"Dynamite. We blow the sonofabitch to kingdom come."

"Uh—right—you got some dynamite?"

"Didn't old Wooden Eye Bishop use to be a powder monkey on the new highway? I bet he's still got some."

"That was a while ago, Smoke. He don't do that no more. Don't forget, he's only got the one hand now."

"He doesn't have to do any of it—I'll do it! He only has to give us the dynamite."

"Since when d'you know how to use powder, huh?"

"Can't be that hard. We've seen it used. We'll get Wooden Eye to give us a few pointers. Where's he at now?"

"Who?"

"Pay attention, Shorty! Wooden Eye!"

Shorty squints into Daddy's face. "Huh? Old

Wooden Eye? Somewhere up around Agate Beach, I guess."

"Think you could find his house?"

"I been there a long time ago when I was surveying with him—might could, I guess."

"Well, okay then. Let's go!"

Mama drops her arms. Her hands slap her hips. She raises her voice. "Delbert! You're not going any- where—it's almost midnight!" No one dares call my daddy by his real name except Mama.

"How many damn weeks do you want to keep smell- ing that?" Daddy stands and puts on his old brown work hat, the one with the brim turned up all around. "C'mon, Shorty, let's go find Wooden Eye."

Shorty tries to stand but flops back into the chair, folds his arms on the table, and puts his head down. "I'm coming, Smoke—"

"Get up, Shorty!" Daddy staggers over to drag Shorty to his feet, gets tangled in Shorty's legs, and lands on his rump on the linoleum.

Mama says, "You're not going anywhere tonight ex- cept to bed. Now, stand up." She grabs him by the arms and pulls, then calls Frankie to help her. They get Daddy, almost asleep and singing his old Irish songs, undressed and into bed. They stretch Shorty out on the floor away from the stove so Mama can start the fire in the morning. She clears the table of the dirty ashtray, the empty jar of pickled pigs' feet, the four brown quart bottles, and the empty glasses.

Mama says to Frankie, "I don't think I can stand much more of this."

I'm still scrunched down behind the door, listening. I get a scared knot in my stomach when I hear Mama sound so sad and mad. I sneak away and crawl into my daybed. Mama hadn't even noticed me hiding behind the kitchen door, watching everything through the crack. She'd put Danny to bed much earlier, and Frankie always stays up as late as he wants, but she didn't even miss me to tell me to go to bed too. That's why I know Frankie is Mama's favorite.

I wake up real early and am still sleepy, until I remember that Goofy'd said he was going down to bury the whale this morning. And he doesn't know that Daddy and Shorty are going to blow it up today! I have to tell him. I have to stop him.

I slide down the bank and run to his shop. Door locked, lights out. I pound on the glass door and holler, "Goofy! Goofy!" No answer. He's left, I know he's left. I run down the sandy road and around the bend toward Jump-off Joe's. The tide's coming in. I see Goofy's long skinny footprints sunk into the sand, and I see Goofy standing between the bank and the whale. His back is turned. He doesn't see me. He has a shovel in his hand. *And there's the whale! Oh! It's huge! Huge!* So is the stink.

I squeeze my nose with my fingers and holler over the crashing of the waves, "Goofy! Wait! I got to tell you something!" He doesn't turn, he doesn't hear me. He begins to dig. I know the sand is drier and softer below the bluff, and I can see now how it is sliding right back into the hole he's just dug. I pinch my nose tighter, take a few steps closer, but the smell of the whale is like a wall. I can't take another step. I scream, "Goofy! It's me, Maggie! Wait! I got to tell you something!"

He turns around to get another shovelful of sand. He sees me and drops the shovel. With both hands he begins to push at the air. He's telling me to go back. But I am frozen to my spot. I know it's Goofy, but he looks so scary, like a monster in his gas mask: black face and bug eyes and a tin can where his nose should be. He's wearing his rusty helmet and those army puttees are hanging from his knees. If he's trying to tell me something, I can't hear a word, for the waves are making too much noise. Then my whole insides begin to slip and slide. I grab my stomach.

He's still waving his arms at me. Then he bends over and yanks the mask off to have one of his coughing fits.

I think he can hear me better now, so I yell again, "Goofy! My daddy's going to blow up that whale! Come on!" Goofy puts his hand behind his left ear and shakes his head. Then he bends over, too busy coughing again to look my way. I leave, I just have to.

When I climb the bank, there goes Daddy and Shorty in the pickup, heading up Oceanview Drive. Agate Beach isn't far from here.

Mama grabs me at the door, shakes me hard by my arm, scolds me for sneaking out, and marches me into the kitchen. She won't listen to me until she hears me cry and say for the fifth time that Goofy is down on the beach trying to bury the whale and that he's wearing that old mask and helmet and having more of those coughing fits.

"Stop crying! What are you saying about Goofy?"

"He's going to bury the whale and he's wearing that old war mask—"

"Oh, no! Did you tell him about the dynamite?"

Now I'm crying harder. "He couldn't h-hear me—I couldn't get close enough because that old whale s-st-stinks, and the ocean was m-m-making too much noise—my stomach hurts—my head hurts—I'm getting s-s-sick."

Mama hugs me. "Don't worry, your daddy and

Shorty will see him, I'm sure. No more crying now, you hear?"

Aunt Fern walks in the back door. She's wearing a red bandanna tied around her face. Only her eyes show. She looks like a real bandit. Then I smell another stink, a familiar one, coming from Fern's bandanna.

"Oh, God, gimme some coffee, please," she says, "I'm out, and everything else tastes rotten."

"Jeez, Jean, how can you stand it?" She pulls down her bandanna and takes the mug of hot coffee Mama has poured for her, puts her nose close to the rim, and sniffs. "Too hot, too hot, smells delicious, though, Jean, thanks, thanks a lot."

Mama gives Fern one of her suspicious looks. "Fern, you been drinking this early? And on a Sunday morning?"

"Who? Me? Oh, that? No, Jean, I just soaked my bandanna in whiskey this morning so I don't have to smell that pile of—you know . . ."

Mama waves at the air but says nothing. Aunt Fern sees all the new bread and sniffs at the loaves. Her nostrils are two huge black holes. She grins at Mama and lifts her eyebrows.

"No, Fern. They're for Smokey's crew. They're coming by sometime today to pick them up. Sorry."

Daddy's crew pays Mama ten cents a loaf, which makes Daddy mad. He wants her to give it to his friends for free. They want to pay. Cigarette money, Mama says.

Aunt Fern, who's really just a neighbor, not my aunt, shrugs and says, "I might just as well go to Mass uptown as stay home and pass out from that rotten . . ."

She sees Mama's dirty look and spies me sitting at the table like I've been invisible until this very minute. "Hey, Maggie, you want to go to Mass with me?"

"Okay. What's a mass?"

"No, Fern, she's not Catholic, and she's not dressed right. You go on by yourself." She gives Fern and me that special look and we both know what it means: I'm at the end of my rope. Don't say another word.

Aunt Fern leaves by the back door and in a few minutes I sneak out the front. I have to see if Goofy has given up and gone back home. I'm so scared, I start chewing on my lower lip, which I do sometimes until it bleeds and I get a scab. I've got to get close enough to the edge of the bluff so I can warn him about the dynamite, just in case Daddy doesn't see him there behind the whale. I hold my nose and walk a little faster. I wish I had a big cowboy bandanna like Aunt Fern's, but without that whiskey smell.

Aunt Fern comes down the sidewalk all dressed up and heading to church. She's still wearing her red bandanna over her nose. She asks where I'm going. I tell her I've got to go warn Goofy. "Wanna come?" I say, hoping she'll say yes. I'm chewing on my lip again. The blood tastes sweet.

"Warn him about what?"

I try to tell Aunt Fern, but my throat seems all closed up. I shake my head and turn away.

Aunt Fern laughs. "Well, swell, what the hell, might as well, never can tell, it's a lousy smell!"

I wonder if Aunt Fern is getting drunk breathing in that whiskey soaked in her bandanna through those big nostrils of hers. I've already pinched my nose practically off my face and keep breathing through my mouth, and here's Aunt Fern acting so cheery and silly, like there's no stinking rotten whale on the beach.

At the metal fence, I say, "We gotta go real slow the rest of the way."

Aunt Fern barges ahead on her high heels. They sink into the soft sandy ground with each step. She teeters right at the edge of Jump-off Joe's.

"Hey! I can see Shorty's old truck down there, and the tide's coming in—the water's almost to the wheels. What the hell is it doing down there? And, hey! There's your dad and Shorty stretching out some kind of wire." Fern bends over to look straight down the bluff. "Is that the whale? Oh, my God! It is the whale! It's all sunk in, I can see its ribs, they're huge! Hey! Wait a minute! I see a shovel half under and, oh, no! I see— a—is that Goofy's leg sticking out from under? Oh— no!"

She stumbles back and grabs on to me. She's crying like a baby. "Maggie! It's Goofy!"

"Goofy? Where?" Aunt Fern has me in her clutches. I try to get away, to run back to the edge, I have to see!

Just then, I hear my daddy shout, "Fire in the hole! Fire in the hole!"

Shorty hollers, "Let's get out of here, Smoke! The tide! It's up to the wheels!" Then the roar of the engine as the old pickup heads around the bend toward the road.

Then what happens? *I don't know!* I hear this huge big boom and I grab my ears. I drop to my knees. The ground beneath my knees begins to shudder and rumble. Then it's rolling, and I'm riding something wild and I can't get off. I hear a million tiny bells ringing in my ears. *And my ears, oh, they hurt me, they hurt me.*

Aunt Fern hollers, "It's the end of the world!"

When the shaking stops, I open my eyes. Dirt and sand are raining down from the sky and Jump-off Joe's is not a bluff anymore, but a long slope that drops in front of our feet and slides into the ocean. Large chunks of sandstone are rolling into the foaming water. The air is churning around me—it looks like thick brown gravy and smells like burnt hamburger.

Aunt Fern holds out her hand. "Oh, Jesus-marries-joseph-and-our-father's-art-is-in-heaven-with-the-lamp-of-God-my-a-cuppa-mya-cuppa-mya-cuppa-oh-my-god-I-am-hardly-sorry-for-having-a-fence-in-the . . ." Her red bandanna is hanging from her left ear.

Something soft and wet plops on my head. I hold out my arms and stare at the gooey blobs raining down on me, landing on my arms. I'm shaking so hard I can't focus my eyes. My hands are floating. They don't belong to my arms anymore. I begin to float too. *Where? Away. Far, far away to someplace else where this could never, never happen.*

Daddy for Sale

I'm right there that afternoon when Aunt Fern tells Mama she wants to buy my daddy for her older sister, Connie. Well, I'm not *right there* in the kitchen. I'm in the front room right next to the kitchen door. I'm leaning up against the side of the daybed where I sleep, cutting out a Betty Boop paper doll from the funny pages so I can trace around to make a paper dress to hook on with those little cutout tabs—the kind you have to fold over just right or the dress will fall off—but I hear everything they say.

It's the day after Mama and me and my two brothers get back home from staying the summer in the valley with Grandma and Grandpa, back to Newport on the night bus, and Daddy not there to meet us like Mama said he would. So we have to walk down the hill to Nye Beach in the dark, carrying our boxes and suitcase, my little brother, Danny, whining to be carried, and Mama saying to me, for God's sake, pick him up. Then she clams up, too busy walking fast to talk to anyone, not even to my big brother, Frankie. The first thing she says when she opens the door and presses in the light button is "Oh, no!"

For the lights don't come on. The house stays dark. I'm still hanging on to little Danny, who's half asleep and heavy, while Mama bumps around in the dark until she finds a candle.

Frankie, who's carrying a heavy box, stumbles over something in the middle of the living room floor that turns out to be Daddy's shoes. Then Mama swears again and finds a match and tells me to make Danny stop crying, and then she lights the candle.

Frankie finds the kerosene lamp we keep for when the storms and lightning blow out all the lights, but this is summertime. There hasn't been any storms. So what's the matter with the lights, I ask Mama? She says for me to keep quiet and sit down with Danny, who's crying louder now and wants her to hold him, not me.

Now that my eyes are used to the candlelight, I see my daybed. I put Danny down and keep patting him on the back and bottom until he calms down. Finally Frankie lights the lantern and carries it into the kitchen, and then he yells for Mama. Me and Mama hurry in and find our daddy lying on the kitchen floor in front of the stove, looking like he's dead. But he isn't dead.

"Dead drunk," Mama says.

Later, when Daddy comes to, he cries and says he's sorry, but that's after Mama finds out he hasn't worked the last two months. She's crying too, and saying she can't take it anymore, and then she tries to drink the Lysol she keeps in the bathroom to clean the toilet with, until Frankie takes the bottle away from her lips before she can drink a single drop.

So when Aunt Fern says she wants to buy my daddy for her older sister, Connie, I listen real hard. I can't figure out why anyone would want him the way he is this morning, his eyes all red and face so gray, drinking eggnog and the hair of the dog with shaky hands, and leaving early to see if he still can have a job working on the jetty they're building in the harbor. So my mama, who spends all morning cleaning the whole house and scrubbing clothes and bedsheets on the washboard and hanging them out on the line, has just put Danny down for a nap and isn't feeling too good herself. She's just sat down at the kitchen table to drink a cup of coffee and have a cigarette and stare out the window when Aunt Fern comes in the back door. She sits too, without being invited, and asks can she have a cup of coffee?

She has something important she wants to talk to Mama about.

I'm glad to hear her voice coming from the kitchen because Aunt Fern lives right next door. She and Mama are neighbors to each other, borrowing things back and forth—except it's usually Aunt Fern doing most of the borrowing. Aunt Fern is funny, making faces and saying funny things and sometimes talking dirty, which Mama doesn't like and says so. But she says Aunt Fern's a character and her heart's in the right place, so for me not to pay any attention, not to pick up any bad habits from Aunt Fern or to listen when she says her dirty words.

One time, after working at the cannery, Aunt Fern is at our house trying out Daddy's new batch of home-made beer. I ask her, "Do you like chocolate-covered cherries, Aunt Fern?"

She answers, "I hope to kiss a cow's—" Then she laughs real loud.

Mama yells, "Fern! You've got no call to be talking filthy like that! Shame on you!"

Aunt Fern hiccups and giggles and burps. "Oops! Sorry. What'd you put in this stuff, Smokey?"

My daddy scowls and says he doesn't appreciate her conducting herself in that manner in front of his children, and if she doesn't know how to hold her liquor like a man, to go home. Otherwise, he's always very friendly with Aunt Fern and also with her older sister, Connie.

When they play three-handed pinochle at the kitchen table, Mama never touches a drop of home brew, which they say makes her a wet blanket. But when Daddy and Aunt Fern laugh at her, it sounds more friendly than mean, like everyone is just having fun.

Aunt Connie, who comes sometimes to be the fourth hand, tells Mama, "Never mind those two. They were always cutting up, never acting their age when we were in school."

"Oh?" Mama says, looking surprised at Daddy. "You never told me you went to school with Connie and Fern."

"I didn't?"

"No, you didn't. How come you never told me?"

Daddy shrugs and begins to shuffle the cards. "Guess I never thought much about it. What of it? Let's play cards." He begins to deal.

Mama keeps looking at Daddy, but he just keeps on dealing.

"We all went to Tillamook High—I thought you knew that," Aunt Connie says.

"No, I didn't know that," Mama says.

"Well, it wasn't any big secret," Daddy says, "you probably just forgot."

"No," Mama says, "I didn't forget."

Aunt Connie says, "It was a long time ago, Jean. We were just kids."

Mama sits looking at her hands. She doesn't touch her cards. Daddy says to her, "Well, are we going to play, or aren't we? Go on! Pick up your cards." But Mama says no, she doesn't feel like playing pinochle anymore. She's sorry, but they will have to count her out. She goes into the bathroom.

So Aunt Connie says to Fern, "It's late. We should be going." She says her boy, George, is home alone. And then Daddy says no, stay, they can play three-handed pinochle, but they leave anyhow.

Aunt Connie's husband, Otto, owns the fish cannery down on the waterfront. They have a big car and a big house on the bluff. She's very pretty and always acts more ladylike than her younger sister. I never feel quite right calling her Aunt Connie, and I never talk to her or see her again after that time when Daddy takes me with him for a walk on the beach and we end up at her house. He tells me to go play in the attic with her son, George, and he'll call me when he's ready to go.

George has lead soldiers and a toy tank that runs

when you wind it with a key, so we play army and forget about his mama and my daddy. George has black hair and black eyes and looks like his mother. My daddy has black hair and black eyes too, but mostly he's getting bald. We're both eight and in the same grade at school.

I've never been in an attic before. I like the long room with the ceiling slanting down on both sides and a window on each end that lets in just enough light for us to see all our soldiers lined up ready to fight each other. George says he gets to have the tank on his side because it's his house, which I don't think is very polite since I'm company. I never played with him at recess because I don't like boys, so I don't really know him. At school I spend most of my time upside down on the bars and rings. I'm always very busy at recess.

When my daddy finally calls me that we're ready to go, I run down all those stairs. When I get to the kitchen door I hear Aunt Connie say, "Maybe it's not a good idea to bring you-know-who along next time."

Daddy sees me standing there and gives me a funny look. He frowns, real serious, and says, "Maggie doesn't tell tales out of school, do you, honey?"

I shake my head "no" and look down at my bare feet.

Daddy musses my hair with his big hand and says, "That's my girl." Which I already know I am.

And I know I have to keep this secret for my daddy, even though I don't want to come back and play any more toy soldiers with selfish George, who wouldn't share his tank.

"Go wait on the porch," Daddy says, "I'll be there in a minute." He closes the door, and I hear Aunt Connie give a little squeal before they're quiet. When he finally comes out he's smiling. He takes my hand, and we walk back up the beach.

Soon after that school is out and Mama takes us on the bus to stay with Grandma and Grandpa, so I'm not around to go walking with my daddy, or keep his secrets. And you already know what happens when we get off the night bus at Newport and Daddy isn't there.

So when Aunt Fern says she wants to buy my daddy for her sister, Connie, that's why I have to listen. But that comes after Mama gives Aunt Fern the cup of coffee. I'm having trouble getting my round-top scissors to cut the pointed spikes in Betty Boop's hair, and I want to go into the kitchen to ask Mama to help me. But when Aunt Fern says she has something important she wants to ask Mama, I can tell by her voice she isn't the same cheery Aunt Fern I'm used to. So I wait. My mama's voice isn't too cheery either, kind of low and tired sounding.

"What?" Mama says.

Aunt Fern says, "I'm not sure how to start—it's kind of a ticklish situation."

"What is?"

"Well," Aunt Fern begins, then asks, "Uh—you got any milk?"

"I thought you drank it black," Mama says.

"I do most of the time, but I had a rough night, and my stomach's feeling like the bottom of the barrel."

So I hear Mama get the milk bottle out of the icebox and put it on the table. It's quiet, which I figure is because Aunt Fern is pouring the milk and stirring her coffee. By this time I've cut off the top of one of Betty Boop's curls, which makes me mad at myself and at Mama for not helping me. I try to trim it with the scissors but Betty Boop's point of hair gets smaller and smaller. I go ahead and trace her body on some paper, getting ready to draw a dress. Aunt Fern's going on about her stomach being queasy isn't very interesting, and it isn't easy tracing a paper doll that's cut out of the newspaper because it's so thin and hard to hold down and trace at the same time.

Mama says something about it's too bad about Aunt Fern's upset stomach, does she have the flu?

And Aunt Fern says, "No, I was up half the night with Connie." Then she asks, "Did Smokey go to work today?"

And Mama says, "Yes—that is, if he still has a job."

"Well, that's good, anyway," Aunt Fern says, like she's not really listening to Mama.

Then I hear my mama start crying and talking at the same time in this squeaky voice, saying, "He didn't pay the light bill, and who knows how we're ever going to get by until payday. I just spent our last dollar on that milk and some bread and beans. He says he hasn't worked for two months. I don't understand what happened. What's he been doing all this time?"

I put my pencil down and hold my breath so's I can hear what my mama's saying through her crying. If she doesn't stop, I'll be crying too. My mama says it's because our eyes are built too close to our bladders.

Aunt Fern's voice is low when she says, "Maybe you shouldn't have stayed away so long, Jean."

Mama sounds mad when she says, "Fern! I *had* to get the kids away from all that drinking. You know it was getting bad, and he promised me he would quit! I thought we could save a little money with me living with my folks for a while. But *what* has he been *doing* all this time?"

Aunt Fern says could she have another cup of coffee

and don't worry about the milk, she has plenty. She'll bring over a whole quart for the kids later.

"That won't be necessary, Fern," Mama says.

Then everything is very quiet, so quiet I can hear Daddy's big brass alarm clock ticking in the bedroom. And I hear the stove lid scrape and know Mama's putting another stick of wood in the stove to keep the coffee hot.

Finally Aunt Fern says to Mama, "Did Smokey tell you that the cannery went belly-up just after you left with the kids?"

"No!"

"Yep! Otto took a powder and no one's seen hide nor hair of him since."

Mama says, "No!" again. "How terrible for Connie—and for you, Fern. If you're not working at the cannery, how have you been getting by?"

"I'm okay, got me a job at Moe's chopping clams. It's Connie I'm worried about."

Now that Mama's stopped crying, I'm beginning to get a little sleepy sitting there in the corner leaning up against my daybed, so I crawl up on top of it holding my Betty Boop and thinking I'll just listen while I'm resting. I quit paying attention until I hear my mama say real loud, "What do you mean? What are you saying to me?" Then I sit up straight and pay attention real hard.

Aunt Fern says, "I said Connie's just found out she's pregnant, and Otto ain't been around for three months."

"What's that got to do with us? What are you trying to tell me?"

"Just what I'm saying, Jean. Otto ain't been around and Smokey has."

"I don't believe this!" Mama's voice is so small when she says this that I know she does believe what Aunt Fern is telling her about Aunt Connie and my daddy. I think about the secret I been keeping about my visit to George's house, and I believe it too. Whatever it means.

"Well, I'm sorry, but you better believe it. She's already missed two periods."

The way Aunt Fern's talking, I can tell there's more to this than what I know, so I listen real hard to what my mama says next.

"Two periods?"

"Yep, two periods."

"Be careful, Fern—you're talking about my husband."

"I know that."

"You mean you're accusing Del, you're saying he and Connie . . . ?"

"Yep. That's very definitely what I'm saying."

"It can't be true. When?"

I could hear Aunt Fern give a big sigh. "Right after you left here."

Then Mama's voice is all muffled, and I know she has her hands over her face or her head is down on her arms on the table, the way I do sometimes when I feel like nothing's going right and will never be right again.

"I can't listen to any more of this."

It sounds like my mama is crying. My throat gets real tight and sore now.

Aunt Fern says, "You've got to listen, Jean, because I have a very important proposition to make to you. So will you please just listen for a minute? And don't say nothing, okay? Not until I'm finished with what I got to say, okay?" I hear her take a deep breath; then she says, "Connie'll give you twenty-five hundred dollars if you'll just take the kids and go back to your folks and let her and Smokey work this thing out. She's got the money, and she don't mean you no harm."

The quick way Mama laughs sounds so scary that I get goose bumps on my arms. She hollers, "You mean you want to *buy* my husband? You must be crazy, both of you, asking a thing like that! How dare you? *Get out of my house!*"

But Aunt Fern stays right there. I hear her talking real slow and gentle, like you do to a little kid who's having a crying spell.

She says, "Listen to me, Jean. You got to know it's all over with you and Smokey. He and Connie have been together all this time you been gone. You probably don't know they were sweethearts when they were in school together. They couldn't help it if they fell in love again. Now she's pregnant with his kid."

"I don't care! Let her get an abortion if she's so damn worried!"

Aunt Fern just says, "You know she can't do that. It's against our religion."

Mama gives that scary laugh again and says, "Oh, swell, it's against your religion, but there's nothing in your religion that says it's not all right to steal another woman's husband and have his baby, is that what you're telling me? Go on, Fern, get out of my house!"

When Mama gets hopping mad like that, all red-faced and shouting, I always get real scared, so I get up off the daybed and go stand by the kitchen door.

I see Aunt Fern hasn't budged out of her chair. She just sits there looking at her empty coffee cup. Mama's fingers are jabbing at her package of Chesterfields. She finally rips the top off and pulls out a cigarette. Her hands are all shaky when she reaches a stick match over to the top of the stove and it pops into flame. She takes a long drag that makes her cheeks hollow and blows out a lot of smoke. She says, real tired, "I thought we were friends."

Aunt Fern says, "We are."

Mama laughs, but she doesn't sound happy when she says, "I've had you as a guest in my home all this time, and this has been going on behind my back? That's not what I call friendship, Fern."

Aunt Fern is quiet. Nobody talks. It's so quiet that now Daddy's alarm clock sounds like it's ticking away right here in the kitchen. I can even hear Danny's little snores from where he's in the bedroom taking his nap. I don't know where Frankie went, but he was gone before Mama got Daddy up to go to work.

Mama says, "If you're such a good friend, why didn't you write me this was going on?"

"How could I? She's my big sister and she loves him. Besides, nobody planned it, Jean. It just turned out this way."

I come in and stand by my mama. She doesn't notice me. She's staring hard at Aunt Fern, who's looking back at her, then down at her coffee cup. "I'm real sorry about all this, Jean, honest I am."

My mama gives that laugh again, and says, "Oh, sure," and smokes some more.

I'm watching Aunt Fern, who reaches into her pocket, takes out a piece of paper, and puts it on the table. She smoothes it out with her hand and pushes it over so it is right in front of Mama.

"What's this?" Mama asks.

"Like I say, it's a check for twenty-five hundred dollars made out in your name."

Mama doesn't touch it, just looks at it for a long time.

"Don't worry. It's good, it won't bounce," Aunt Fern says. "Connie has her own account. Otto took the car and cleaned out what was left in the cannery account, but she's got the house and her own money."

Mama pushes the check back to Fern. "I'm not taking this. You take it back," she says.

Fern pushes it toward Mama. "Jean! Don't be a fool. That's a lot of money. Take it. It'll give you and the kids a fresh start. You can go back to your folks and be clear of this whole mess."

So Mama takes the check and holds it in her hands like she's studying every letter in every word and every number real slow. The paper is a pretty pink color. I can read the date and amount and Aunt Connie's name written in purple ink at the bottom. There's a little circle above the "i" instead of the dot my teacher says you're supposed to make.

Then Mama slowly shakes her head at Fern and tears the check in half, puts the two pieces together, and tears it and tears it until the tiny pink and purple pieces fall in a heap in front of her on the table.

Aunt Fern looks at the pile of paper scraps and stands up. "Well, okay," she says, shaking her head. "You can't blame a person for trying."

After Aunt Fern goes out the back door Mama just sits with her head in her hands, staring at all those scraps. I'm looking too, wondering why Mama would do such a thing. I know that a paper check can be the same as real money, but this check is in all these little tiny pieces that can never be put back together again. So what is my Mama going to do now? I don't dare ask. I just watch.

Well, she scoops up that pile of torn pieces and lifts the lid on the stove and lets those little scraps of paper slip through her fingers real slow. Except the little scraps don't just float down nice and easy into the fire but are sucked right into the flames and disappear.

Big Boy Now

Danny sits in front of their new house beside the brand-new highway. His brown legs and bare feet dangle above the drainage ditch. A car zooms lickety-split around the bend. Tires squeal on the hot asphalt, spraying a quick wind of gravel, missing him and Maggie by a whisker. But Danny isn't afraid. He knows he's safe. Nothing can hurt him as long as Maggie has her strong arm around his shoulders. She's wearing a black wool bathing suit with the cutouts under the arms. She's rolled hers down to her bare waist, so he's done the same with his. They are brown as berries from playing on the beach each day since they moved to this cabin court at Tillicum Beach.

The breeze off the ocean is soft. It hardly stirs the cowlick that sprouts from the top of his dark head. There's not a single rain cloud in the whole sky. It is as blue as his brother Frankie's eyes. The sun is hot. Mama calls this Indian summer. But then she says today is Labor Day. He doesn't know which, but he really doesn't care.

Lots of cars are heading down the coast this afternoon. Most of them have yellow-and-black license plates. Rich people are hurrying back to California, where his mama says they should've stayed in the first place. The brand-new highway, named after Mr. Lincoln, is also yellow and black—black as a licorice whip. Or a water snake with a yellow stripe down its back, the kind Danny saw yesterday swimming on top of the water in this very ditch. He gives a quick look but sees no snake today.

Another car speeds by. He looks down the road and sees it turning all shimmery and watery. It's being swallowed up by what Maggie calls a mirage, which means that the car isn't really floating on water—it just gets its tires wet. Maggie, who's almost nine, is his teacher. She's always learning him how to do things, like today when she's learning him how to count.

"There goes twenty-nine! I saw it first," she hollers.

"There goes twenty-nine! I saw it first," he hollers.

"Here comes thirty! You did not!"

"Here comes thirty! Did too!"

"Did not!" She takes her arm away from around his shoulders.

"Did too!" He pokes out his lower lip and places her warm arm back where it was. "Here comes thirty-sixty! I saw it first!" he shouts. He's grinning at her now.

She gives him a disgusted look. "That's not California. That's Oh-ree-gon." She drags out the word "Oregon." It makes him feel bad—he's made a mistake. He scowls and grabs a handful of gravel and throws it at the highway.

"I knew that."

"Besides, thirty-sixty isn't even a number," she says.

"I knew that."

"Well, if you knew it, do it right."

"I will. I meant thirty-twenty."

She shakes her head and sighs. "You're never going to learn."

"I am too." He throws two more handfuls of gravel and watches the chunks bounce and scatter across the road. He doesn't care anymore about counting any old license plates or not being old enough to go to school tomorrow. She can go without him—see if he cares. And his big brother, Frankie—him too. Let them get to ride the yellow school bus. Mama says he's lucky because he gets to stay home with her all day.

Another car rushes by too close, sending gravel flying toward them. Maggie grabs him and holds him tight.

She brushes away the gravel he's holding in his hand. "Don't do that anymore," she says.

One old truck, with muddy license plates and a stack of wooden berry flats bouncing in the back, lumbers by, heading north.

"Thirty-ten! I saw it first!" he hollers. Again he grins, showing her a mouthful of baby teeth.

"Doesn't count. Can't you see it's going the wrong way? Besides, you can't tell if it's from California when it's covered with all that mud. You gotta use your eyes and use your brain."

"I do," he says.

"You gotta use it all the time, not just once in a while."

"I do," he says again.

Maggie begins to drop gravel one piece at a time into the drainage ditch below their feet, making little splashes in the water, where she says the salamanders live.

"Salamanders get fat and have babies," she said.

He peers between his feet into the water, hoping to see a live salamander swim by. He's never actually seen one in the water, but Maggie caught one once and kept it in a quart mayonnaise jar. It was brown on top and had a very fat orange belly. Mama said it looked like it was going to have babies, but it died before that happened.

He bends closer and squints into the ditch. "Where are the babies?"

"The mama keeps them hidden in little caves under the water until she can teach them how to swim."

"What does she feed them?"

"She feeds them little marshmallows. They roast them on little tiny sticks over a little tiny fire in front of their cave way down at the bottom of the ditch."

He gives her a look that says now she's the one not using her brain. He says, "You can't light a fire in water."

She smiles and gives him a poke. "You're right! Now you're using the old noggin."

"I know. You can't light a fire in water 'cause the match would go out. So how does the baby salamanders roast their marshmallows?"

"They don't. They eat 'em raw."

"I like mine roasted better," he says. "I wish we had some marshmallows right now." He hears his stomach growl.

"There goes thirty-one!" She's caught him off guard.

"That's no fair." He hadn't even seen the big black car with its yellow-and-black license plates coming around the bend, but now he sees the little boy waving at him from the back window. He doesn't wave back. "I don't want to play this anymore." He stands up.

"Don't whine. You want to learn how to count past thirty, don't you?"

He shrugs. "I'm hungry."

She pulls him down beside her and puts her arm around him again, smiling in that secret way that means she's going to tell him something he doesn't know. She says, "Californians have big cars and lotsa money."

"I already know that." She's told him this before. He tries to stand, but she holds him down.

"And—and—they get to eat ice cream every day!"

His brown eyes grow big and shiny. He grins and nods his head. "Yeah, they get to eat ice cream every day." He remembers the time not too long ago when they were moving here from Newport. At the Waldport bus depot, he got to have ice cream! He had to dig it out of the small paper tub with a wooden spoon, and the spoon was so flat that sometimes the little swirl of ice cream missed his mouth and landed in the dirt at his feet.

"When I get big, I'm going to have me a big shiny car and I'm going to eat ice cream every day."

"You don't get to do that."

"How come?"

"Because you're not from California."

"How do you get to be from California?"

"You don't. You gotta be born there."

"What do they do in California?"

She says, "Nothing. They just drive around all day in their big black shiny cars."

"And eat ice cream every day." His stomach growls again.

He jumps when he hears his mama shout, "You kids get out of that ditch and away from that highway! You want to get yourself killed? Didn't I tell you to go play down on the beach? Maggie, what's the matter with you? How many times have I told you not to play in front of the house? Those big cars don't even see you sitting there by that ditch—all they have to do is swerve and you'd be dead! I'm ashamed of you! You're supposed to be taking care of your little brother!"

"I am."

"You're not! I asked you to do one little thing for me. Danny, get over here right now!"

He stands and brushes the gravel from his bottom and begins to tiptoe through the weeds and stickers. His mama is standing at the corner of the house, her left hand resting on her hip. In the right hand she holds a green-handled toilet plunger, which she is shaking like a stick.

"I didn't do it," Danny says to himself, and keeps his eyes on the dirt and weeds. He can't stand to look at the plunger in her hand. It means that Mrs. Jones, who owns the six small cabins in the court, has made his mama clean the stopped-up toilet again.

He's heard her tell his mama, "He done it again, that little boy of yourn, he done used too much paper. Now there's a mess of dirty water and I ain't saying what else is all over that cement floor. When ya gonna teach him how to wipe hisself without usin' half a roll? There's lotsa men has to use that toilet. Yo' ain't the only ones live here, you know, and they work hard in the woods all day. They don't cotton to be comin' home and findin' no mess your little boy's made. I swear, some people is better off with outhouses and a Monkey Wards catalog!" Then Mama looks real mad, and gets tears in her eyes, and she goes and gets that red-and-green plunger.

A car honks as it speeds by. His mama gives a mean look down the highway. "Damn Californians," she says. "Why don't you go back to where you come from, and stay there?"

"Ouch! Ouch! Ouch!" he says, and begins to hop. He's got a sticker in his big toe. He hears his mother laugh and sees the tears in her eyes, a different kind of tears now, so he laughs too, and dances toward her on the sides of his feet to show how brave he is. He clutches her around the legs and hugs her hard. Then she lifts him to her hip as if it doesn't matter that the damp wool of his bathing suit is soaking into her thin housedress, or that he's getting too big to be carried. He rides her hip like a pony ride when she walks to the back of the cabin and puts him down on a tree stump to look for the sticker in his big toe.

She drops the plunger to the ground. "I don't see it."

"It's right there." He sticks his leg in the air and puts his finger on the spot. He can feel the sharp prick when he presses. "Ouch!"

"Move your hand," she says, and gently rubs her finger back and forth over the toe.

"Ouch! Ouch! Ouch!" he cries again, and pushes her hand away.

"Maggie, go in the house and get my tweezers."

He holds his breath while his mother removes the sticker and kisses his toe, which makes him laugh again. Again he sees the tears in her eyes when she smiles and pretends she's going to eat his whole foot, dirt and all.

"Now, you two do what I say, go play down on the beach."

And so, following his big sister, he flies down the path like a wild bird, his wings outstretched, expecting his toes to leave the ground any minute, ready to lift off into the blue sky and the warm sun that fills the ocean with winking lights so bright he can hardly look without it hurting his eyes. When his bare feet hit the hot sand, he has to fold his wings and slow to a walk; then he dances again, hopping now onto the small pieces of driftwood and dried seaweed scattered like stepping-stones on the beach. Slowly he makes his way toward the silver-gray logs piled high by last winter's storms. Maggie is already in their hideout.

"Hurry up!" she orders. "Come on!"

"I can't," he says, and waits. She always helps him climb, then slide down the smooth wood into the dark hole.

"Sure you can."

"You come get me."

"No, you can do it yourself. You're a big boy now."

She says that when she wants to teach him something new. He feels his knees tingle and his chest thump. He begins to run around the shiny logs looking for a toe-hold, a knothole or a branch to grab on to. He finds what he needs, a notch in the wood, and climbs up the slanting gray log on all fours. "I'm a monkey—see?" he says to the sky.

"See, I told you you could do it." Maggie's voice comes from the dark cave beneath the mountain of logs.

Soon he slides into their hideout. He wriggles himself a rump hole in the cool sand.

Maggie says, "I know what we can do."

"What?"

"We can smoke. You wanna smoke?" Her new big teeth are white and square and her brown eyes are shining and sharp. He doesn't dare look away or let her know how much she scares him sometimes.

"I don't know how."

"That's okay. I'll teach you. It's easy."

"How do you know? Did you already do it?"

"Not with a whole cigarette, but I been watching Mama and Daddy."

"But we don't got no cigarettes," he says slowly.

"That's okay. I know where to get some."

"Where?"

"On the dresser in the bedroom. Daddy's Bull Durham. You go and get it and bring it here." Her eyes are still shining, warm and friendly, but he feels a sudden chill between his legs. He shakes his head.

"Huh-uh! I ain't gonna do that."

"You said you would."

"I did?"

"Yes, you promised. You gave your word."

"I did not say I promise—"

But now he isn't sure. He never can remember exactly what he's said, but Maggie *always* remembers.

"You said, okay, and that's the same thing. You don't want to be called a liar, do you?"

"N-No."

"Don't you know that when you give your word, that's sacred? You can't change it even if you have to die." She's scowling at him from under her dark eyebrows. She looks just like Daddy. Daddy's the one who told him never to tell a lie and to always keep your word—but which word? Daddy says a lot of words. And if every word is sacred, then he's going to have to try to remember them all, even if he forgets and has to ask again.

"What's 'sacred' mean?"

"What's 'sacred' mean?" She stares at him in the dim light, scowling again. He can't tell if she's thinking about it, or mad at him for asking.

"Maggie! What's 'sacred' mean?"

"It means you gotta do what you said you'd do, like how you promised to go get Daddy's Bull Durham off the dresser. So, go get it!"

Now he knows he has to do it. He has to go get the white bag of tobacco with the yellow string and the little blue package of brown cigarette papers stuck on its side. He stands up and wipes the sand from his rump.

"And don't let Mama see you," Maggie warns. "Just sneak in and sneak out. You can do it. Didn't I tell you you're a big boy now?"

She boosts him out of the hole and he picks his way up and down and over the mountain of silver-gray logs until his feet are on hot sand again.

"Don't forget the matches," she calls in a loud whisper.

He runs across the sand and up the path into the darkened woodshed. He listens at the back door, then opens it a crack and peeks in. The kitchen is empty. So is the living room. He tiptoes across the linoleum and peers into the bedroom. It's empty, too. Where's Mama? Where's Frankie?

"Mama?" he says in a small voice.

There's no answer. He's alone. He puts his hand on the bed and gently rubs the chenille cover, soft like Mama's skin. The bedspread is smooth and pulled up over the pillows in the neat way his mother does things. He looks under the bed, sees the enamel night jar, Mama's flannel slippers. In the corner stand Daddy's cork boots—his logger boots. They are black and oily and have sharp nails sticking out of the bottoms. His work pants and black wool underwear are hanging on the hook behind the door. This means Daddy didn't go to work today, didn't come home again last night.

The suspenders hang like wide belts from what his daddy calls his tin pants. They remind him of the leather razor strap his daddy uses to sharpen his razor when he shaves, the one he also uses on Frankie when he's bad. Then he spots the sack of Bull Durham on the dresser next to Mama's hairbrush and a box of stick matches. He grabs the sack and matches and runs.

"What kept you?" she scolds when he slides into their hiding place. "Gimme that!" She grabs the sack and slips a thin piece of brown paper from the blue envelope. She curls the paper between two fingers and hands him the pouch. "Open this," she orders.

His fingers shake when he loosens the yellow string and gives her the sack. He watches her sitting cross-legged and crouched as she tips the pouch and pours the tobacco onto the paper trough.

"You're doing it just like our daddy," he says.

He admires the way she takes the unrolled cigarette and brings it to her lips, licks the edge of the paper, then rolls the two edges together. The edges won't meet. He can see the cigarette is too fat.

"You got too much tobacco," he says.

"I know." She knocks some onto the sand.

"You need more spit," he says.

"I know." She sucks on her mouth, gets more spit on her tongue, and again licks the edge of the paper. The cigarette begins to droop and spill tobacco onto her bare feet.

"You spilled it, and you got tobacco on your tongue."

"I know it!" she says between clenched teeth, and begins to spit and blow the sticky strands of tobacco from her lips. She crushes the soggy mass into a ball and tosses it away. She reaches for another paper.

"You got tobacco on your teeth."

"Shut up!" She carefully pours a smaller trail of tobacco onto the paper trough. This time, when she wets it and brings the edges together, they meet and stick, but the skinny cigarette collapses in the middle and the brown, hairy tobacco pokes out each end. She throws down the sticky mess and yells at him, "Go get Mama's Chesterfields!"

His voice is very small. "I don't wanna."

"Yes, you do! Now, go get 'em!"

"No. I don't wanna smoke."

"You don't have to! I'll do the smoking! You just go get 'em!" Her strong hands are clenched into fists now and her black brows are hanging over her eyes again. He feels his lower lip tremble and pull at the corners.

Then she smiles and takes his hand. "You can do it. I know you can. You're a big boy now, remember?"

He lets out a little sigh. As always, she's right. He knows he can do it, he's done it once already. It's safe. No one is home. He knows where Mama keeps her Chesterfields, right there on the counter beside the bread box. He gives his sister a quick grin and taps his front tooth.

The tide is coming in and the sand is cooler on his feet. The crashing of the breakers excites him, makes him feel strong. He isn't afraid of the ocean. He isn't afraid of anything. He feels like singing. "Go get Mama's Chetter-fields, Chetter-fields, Chetter-fields!" he sings to the trees and to the beat-up trailer resting on chunks of sawed logs beside the path. He hears loud voices in the trailer. Phinola the Indian and her Swede husband are fighting again, saying bad words he isn't supposed to hear, words his daddy says only when he's mad or drunk. Mama says that when Phinola drinks too much beer she goes outside and runs her head straight into a tree.

In the woodshed he stops to catch his breath, then opens the back door a crack. Just like the last time, the house is quiet. He can sneak in, grab Mama's cigarettes, and run all the way back to the hiding place. But his stomach hurts and he has goose bumps on his arms and legs. He looks around the dark woodshed. There, stuck in the chopping block, is the double-edged ax Frankie uses to cut the morning kindling. The wood is stacked in a neat pile beside the back steps. When he gets big he's going to do that for his mama too, just like Frankie.

But first he has to keep his sacred promise to his sister. He opens the door. The cigarettes are waiting for him right there on the counter next to the bread box. He takes the pack in its shiny cellophane wrapper and turns toward the back door. Then he freezes. There are voices coming from the bedroom. He can hear his mother! She's crying, and his big brother is pleading with her.

"Don't cry, Mama, please don't cry—it's going to be all right—everything is going to be all right. . . ." His brother's voice cracks.

"Now, don't you start crying," he hears his mama say.

"I can't help it. I can't stand to see you cry!"

"I just don't know how long we can go on like this. Where is he? Why does he keep doing this? Doesn't he know he's destroying the family?"

"I hate him! I hope he never comes back."

"Oh, Frankie, no. You mustn't say those things—

he's your father. It'll get better, you'll see. Now, please, just go get me my cigarettes."

Frankie's coming! Danny squeezes into the corner by the stove, his eyes closed, hugging himself and the pack of Chesterfields in his hand.

He hears Frankie shout, "What are you doing here?" He opens his eyes and there's Mama standing in the doorway behind Frankie.

"What is it? Oh, no! Stealing my cigarettes?" She slumps against the wall.

Danny runs to her and holds out the package. "Maggie made me do it!" he cries, and drops it, spilling cigarettes around his feet. "I didn't want to, Mama! She made me."

He's kneeling, his eyes on his mother's face while his hands fumble over the gray linoleum to find the cigarettes.

His big brother towers above him. "Why do you always have to cause so much trouble? Get out of here!"

Danny grabs on to his mama's legs. "I'm sorry, Mama, I'm sorry."

But she doesn't lean over to pick him up and let him ride her hip, or even to touch his head with her hand. Finally he hears her say, "Go get your sister."

He runs out of the kitchen and through the woodshed. He runs under the black trees past the trailer and onto the sand.

"You've got to come home right now, Maggie! Mama wants you!" he screams. Then he falls to his knees and sobs at the ocean, "Mama is crying! Mama is crying!"

His big sister crawls out of their secret hiding place and runs toward him. "What's the matter? What happened?"

He can't answer. He's pounding his head with his fists, harder and harder, to make the sound of his mama's crying go away.

Maggie kneels before him and grabs his wrists and holds them fast to his sides. She looks into his face. "What's wrong with you?"

"I'm bad, I'm bad, I'm bad!"

"No, no, you're not!" She puts her arms around him and hugs him hard, but he makes himself stiff as a stick. He doesn't want to feel her strong arms and warm skin against his own chill. "You made me do it," he cries, and pushes her away.

She lets him go and sits, her back hunched, scraping and smoothing a spot of sand between her legs until it's wet and cold and gray. With her finger, she digs in the letter "M," then stares at her initial. In one quick stroke of her hand, she brushes it out. She stands, turns her back to him, and crouches low.

"Climb on, Danny," she says. "I'll give you a piggy-back ride."

For a moment he isn't sure. Then he wraps his arms around her neck and places his shivering legs around her waist. She hoists him up on her back, and slowly she carries him across the sand.

Milk Toast for Supper

Danny listens to the pan of milk sizzle on the back of the stove. No one is talking—not Mama, not Frankie, not Maggie. He climbs up on the bed and waits for supper. The bed is practically in the kitchen, in the space his mama calls the alcove. It is next to the door to the woodshed, where Frankie gets spanked with Daddy's razor strap for losing his new jacket again, or for forgetting something else he was supposed to remember. Frankie always cries that he's sorry and won't ever do it again, and begs, "Please, Daddy, don't hurt me—" But then Frankie forgets. Danny squeezes his eyes shut real tight and covers his ears so he can't hear when Frankie gets it. Sometimes Daddy uses a switch or a piece of kindling instead of his razor strap. They make different sounds when they hit. It's always dark in the woodshed.

The bulb hanging over the table is very bright. It

makes the red oilcloth shine like new paint. The floor is full of tiny black nail holes made by loggers' boots. Mama waxes the linoleum lots of times, but the black holes won't go away. That's because loggers' boots have nails sticking out the bottoms so they don't slide off slippery logs. When Daddy comes home from work, he wears his boots in the house, like the other loggers did who lived here before us. His daddy's not at work today, and he's not at home. He hasn't come home for three nights. Mama's eyes are puffy and red.

She puts three bowls of milk toast on the table. She says, "Eat your supper and get into bed. You have school tomorrow." She means Maggie and Frankie, who are almost nine and twelve. They are going to another new school. But not Danny. He's four. Too young, his mama says.

"Come on, Danny, eat now before it gets cold." He picks up a big spoon and does what his mama says. He keeps his eyes on the spoon with its soggy toast and melted butter floating in the hot milk, so he won't spill. Finished, he takes off his clothes, except his BVDs, and climbs into bed. He's a good boy. Mama never has to tell him to do anything twice.

"I'm not going to bed," Frankie says to Mama. "I'm going to stay up again and wait with you." His voice crackles.

Mama tells him, "No, no, no, you *must* sleep tonight! You need your rest." Then she looks at him real hard. "You remember what you're to tell Maggie's teacher if she asks where we live?"

He nods. "I say we live behind Jimmy Mullen's house."

"Yes, and be sure to say we live *inside* the boundary line. You won't forget?"

"I won't."

She looks at him for a minute. "You're sure, now?"

"I'm sure."

Frankie has to tell a lie because Mama is sneaking Maggie on the school bus so she can go to the town school with Frankie. Only junior-high and high-school kids get to take the bus into town. All the younger kids have to go to school at the logging camp. Mama doesn't think it's fair that Maggie should have to go to the one-room schoolhouse at Camp One. She says the teacher is a nineteen-year-old girl whose only ambition is to go to Hollywood and become a movie star. Mama says, "I guarantee you, the only thing those kids will learn this year is how to tap-dance and sing 'Shuffle Off to Buffalo.' No, thank you! Maggie doesn't need to learn that kind of nonsense—she's too smart for that—and she makes enough racket as it is."

Danny tries to say he wants to go to school with

Maggie, but the warm milk and Mama's tired, draggy voice make him sleepy. He hears his own whiny voice say, "Maggie? C'mon . . ." and rolls to the middle of the bed. She undresses to her underwear and crawls over him to the far side, next to the wall. He pushes his bottom into her warm side and begins to doze. He jerks awake when Frankie sits down hard on the side of the bed and begins to untie his shoes. After he has stripped to his undershorts and socks, he rolls under the covers next to Danny.

Maggie says real loud, "Pee-you! Your feet stink!"

Frankie hollers, "You just shut your mouth!"

Danny, in the middle, cries, "Don't let in the cold air!"

Frankie mutters, "Shut up."

Maggie says, "Be quiet!" and hugs Danny.

Mama says, "Now, now, that's enough out of all of you," and turns out the light.

Danny feels Frankie's body shake like he just got out of the freezing ocean. It's warm in Maggie's arms. He yawns and begins to doze again. It's quiet. He smells his mama's cigarette and knows she's sitting right there next to them at the kitchen table, smoking in the dark. He's warm and he's safe.

* * *

The kitchen light snaps on. He hears the shuffling of heavy shoes, but his eyes won't open. The light is too bright. The blankets are whipped off him. He shivers and scrambles to reach for the blankets, but they are thrown over the foot of the bed.

His daddy is talking. "Look at 'em, boys, aren't they beautiful? See 'em? These are my three beautiful children. Look at 'em all cuddled up like that. Didn't I say they were beautiful?"

"That you did, Smokey, you did that, for sure."

"Yup, you shure right dere, Smoke. Dey vera, vera bootiful."

Danny opens his eyes and stares up at three large men standing beside the bed. One is his daddy. He can tell by the way Frankie and Maggie are lying on their backs just as stiff as he is that they are wide awake too. His stomach lurches from the sour smell of whiskey.

His daddy points at him and smiles. "See this little one? He's quite the singer. Stand up, son, and sing for my friends."

Danny shakes his head and puts his pillow over his face. The men laugh. Daddy scowls. He tells Maggie to stand up and sing for his friends. "No!" she says. "I'm not going to do that." She rolls over and turns her back to them.

His daddy pokes his big brother with a stiff finger.

"Well, I know this one will. Stand up here and sing us a song like a man."

Frankie crawls out of bed and says, "I don't know what to sing." He crosses his hands in front of himself, like he doesn't want to show his underwear.

"Stand up straight like I taught you. Sing "Grandfather's Clock.'"

Frankie stands stiff and straight and presses his hands to his sides. Danny can see that he is almost as tall as the man who talks funny. The room is cold. Frankie's knees are shaking. Danny holds his breath. Then his brother begins to sing. The song is slow and sad. Danny's throat hurts as he listens, for Frankie's voice sounds so lonesome. He sings three verses and doesn't forget a single word. One of the strangers blows his nose on a blue bandanna. The other one drags his coat sleeve under his long red nose. Tears run down his daddy's cheeks.

Frankie finishes singing. His daddy looks proud. Each man smiles and gives his brother a nickel. Frankie is still shivering when he gets back into bed and puts his nickels under his pillow. One of the men pats him on the knee, then reaches across Danny to give Maggie a pat. She sits up and yells, "Quit it!"

Danny hears his mama's voice coming from the other room. It sounds like the creaking of a rusty hinge.

Suddenly she's there beside the bed. "Keep your filthy hands off my children and get out of my house, you drunks!" She snatches the blankets and throws them back. Frankie and Maggie tug them up to their chins. Danny is covered again.

"I said get out!" his mama hollers.

"I think we've upset the lady of the house, Smokey. My apologies, Missus," says the shorter man.

"Oh, please, just go." She's not hollering now. It's more like she's begging.

Then his daddy growls. "Now, just a damn minute here. You can't insult my friends like that. They gave me a ride home. I invited them in for a little hospitality. You don't want them to think you don't like them." He tries to put his arm around her. She pushes him away.

"The hell I don't! I *don't* like them—get them out of my house!"

Danny hugs the cold blankets around his ears. The four grown-ups are all bunched up right there between the table and his bed. Now the two strangers are looking sideways at Mama with silly grins on their faces. She is barefoot and wearing a thin nightie. She has goose bumps on her arms and two hard knobs poke out from those soft round pillows on her chest. Daddy is wheezing and trying to focus his eyes on his mama's face. She goes to the sink and says to the window,

"Please. Go home. Can't you see we got enough trouble?" She runs water into the coffeepot and puts it on the stove. She grabs sticks of kindling, lifts the front lid, and jams them into the firebox. Danny listens to the crackling of the fire. He usually likes that sound. Other times. Not now.

The two men drag their feet and shuffle toward the back door. One touches the brim of his hat. "Please pardon the intrusion, Missus."

"Yah, me too," says the other one. Danny hears them stumble through the dark woodshed. A car door slams, an engine cranks up, the car moves out of the driveway. The new fire sizzles in the stove.

Danny takes a deep breath. He has an urge to pee, but he decides he can hold it. The bed is nice and warm again.

Daddy is swaying back and forth beside the bed. "See what you did? You drove my friends away." He sits down at the table and holds his head in his hands.

Mama says, "Some friends. You get a ride into town for a can of peas and condensed milk and you don't come home for three days. Where have you been all this time?" Danny can tell she's crying.

Daddy begins to sing in a low voice, an old Irish tune. Danny usually loves to listen because his daddy sings his name, Danny boy. But not this night.

Mama finds her slippers and goes outside to get milk and three eggs from the cooler nailed to the spruce tree in back of the woodshed. From the cupboard, she takes the can of nutmeg and the little brown bottle of vanilla. Danny watches her as she uses the eggbeater on the eggs and puts in lots of sugar and the other stuff while she warms the milk on the stove. Daddy likes his eggnog hot and real sweet. She pours him a glass and a cup of coffee for herself, smokes, and stares out the window at the black night. Daddy hums as he swallows. He wipes the foam from his upper lip and puts his head on the table.

"No, no, don't go to sleep here," she says. She kneels to untie his shoes and slip them off his feet. "Come on, you've got to go to work in the morning." She turns out the light and leads him from the kitchen through the front room into their small bedroom.

Danny lies there in the dark, staring at the ceiling. There is no sound coming from the bedroom. His eyelids are heavy. He yawns and turns his back to his big sister. She pats him on the shoulder and puts her arm around him. "Go to sleep now," she whispers. "Everything is all right."

Frankie tosses. Under his breath, he says, "That bastard!"

Maggie asks, "Who?"

"Who do you think, stupid?"

"Don't talk to me. You're going to wake up Danny."

"No, he's not. I'm already awake."

Frankie yanks on the blankets and turns over on his side. But Maggie clings to her side, and the blankets settle again. Then all is quiet.

∗ ∗ ∗

It's still dark when Danny feels a rush of cold air and the blankets slipping off his shoulders. The bed squeaks, the mattress moves, and two large feet push themselves between him and Frankie. A sharp toenail scrapes him under his chin. What is it? Is it the Boogie Man? It is the Boogie Man! He's coming to get me! "Mama! Help!"

Her voice comes from the other end of the bed. It's almost a whisper, it sounds far away. "It's all right, honey. I'm right here. Go back to sleep." Her hand finds his foot and gives it a gentle pat.

"Okay." He rolls over so that his mama's cold feet are against his back, not his chest. He wonders what she's doing here in his bed. But he doesn't ask. He's glad she's there. Thinking of the Boogie Man scares him, makes him shiver. Maggie's head is under the blankets. Her body is warm. He can hear her breathing and feel her warm breath. He tucks his head under too. Soon he is warmed by his own breath and stops shivering. He closes his eyes. He hears his mama blow her nose. He squeezes his eyes tighter. He hears the windows rattle. It's raining outside. Maggie and Frankie have stayed asleep. He wants to sleep too. "Mama?"

"I'm right here. Go to sleep, honey."

"Okay, Mama," he says, and closes his eyes.

✳ ✳ ✳

In the morning, just like every other morning, he hears the fire humming in the stove. He opens his eyes and smiles. The kitchen is full of sunshine. He's forgotten his bad dream about the hairy Boogie Man. Then he feels the damp sheet beneath him and says to himself, *I didn't do it*. He knows for sure he didn't. It was Frankie. Frankie acts like he doesn't like him, but that doesn't matter. He knows why Frankie's blue eyes are always sad. Nobody wants to wet the bed. There's something wrong with Frankie. He calls, "Mama?" No answer. He wanders through the other room and looks into their bedroom. No Mama. Sheets and blankets are piled in a corner. The same pee smell fills this room. Mama explained to him once that Frankie and Daddy have very small bladders, but it only happens to Daddy when he gets drunk.

There's the dishpan on the floor next to Daddy's side of the bed. His daddy's been sick again, and now he's gone and his boots are gone. His sister and brother are gone too, and so is Mama. He runs to the kitchen and sees the cereal bowls in the sink. Mama's coffee cup and ashtray are sitting on the table, but her package of Chesterfields is gone.

Then he remembers. Daddy has gone to work. Maggie and Frankie have gone to school. Mama has gone to have a cup of coffee with Phinola, the Indian lady who lives with Jeff, her Swede husband, in the trailer behind Danny's cabin. Phinola calls Danny her little papoose. Until he learned better, he called her Shinola. She's the one who doctored him and Maggie when they first moved to Tillicum Beach, and Daddy got his job as donkey engineer at Camp One. When their first sunburns peeled, Mama rubbed their backs with butter and yellow cream from the top of the milk bottle. Maggie and he went back on the beach too soon and got burned much worse the second time. His back was a bunch of sagging water blisters that Mama poked with a burnt needle—then she almost fainted. Later Maggie got three boils on her back that looked like little volcanoes with yellow peaks. Mama took Maggie to Phinola for help and pinned her down on Phinola's bed while

Phinola's thumbs pressed the lumps and Maggie screamed, "Help! Murder! Police! She's killing me!"

He takes off his BVDs and puts on his black wool bathing suit. The sun is out, but he can't go down on the beach without Maggie. He fixes himself a piece of white bread with butter, sprinkles a heaping spoonful of sugar on it, and walks out the front door into the yard. He tiptoes around the sticker weeds toward the drainage ditch. Mama told them never to sit beside the new highway, but Mama can't see him from Phinola's trailer. Besides, he's not going anywhere. He's just going to wait for Maggie's school bus.

The sun is warm on his bare shoulders. He sits on the edge of the ditch and leans over to see how much water is down there. He gets a sudden urge to pee, stands, and hops up and down. He grabs and wangles his fingers inside a leg of his bathing suit to pull out his stiff wee wee quick, quick! while his other hand balances the slice of sugar bread. He aims his pee at the water in the ditch, but it flies over the ditch and lands past the gravel on the asphalt highway. He looks up and down the road to see if he's been caught, but there is not a single car in sight. And no yellow bus. He gives a big sigh.

Then he remembers, and he laughs out loud. He held

his pee all night! He sits his rump on a spot of dirt, hangs his feet in the ditch again, then takes his first bite from the sugar bread. He chews slowly. He swallows the sweet soggy lump and takes another bite. Then he watches up the road for Maggie's bus.

She will come. He can wait.

The Year I Steal

The year I turn ten I steal all my Christmas presents from the Sprouse Reitz five-and-dime on Main Street. But before I tell you why, I have to tell you what happened.

When Mama got the news from the Greyhound bus driver that her daddy, my grandpa, had just died of a heart attack, she packed up me and my two brothers and we moved to the valley to live with our grandma. The bad part is we left Daddy without him knowing it, because he was somewhere down the coast looking for a job in the woods. The logs were gone at Camp One, and the logging company was moving to Siletz. Daddy hadn't been hired for the next job because he was black-balled for trying to get his friends to join the new union, called the CIO, just getting started in the woods. He was wearing his new white union button on his work hat when he left us, hiking down the road in the rain.

Just before Daddy was blackballed, we had moved from the cabin court at Tillicum Beach to a small beach cottage down the road that didn't even have a name— just an empty bunch of highway someplace closer to Yachats than anywhere. There wasn't a single neighbor in sight. Mama called it "even more godforsaken than the last place." But she said it was cheaper and closer to the one-room camp school, where I had to go now. I hiked through the woods in the rain to learn to tap-dance and sing alto from the nineteen-year-old teacher, Miss Pollard, who put her tap shoes on after she got to school, and clicked all day while she walked. I loved that sound and begged Mama for a pair of tap shoes, but when Christmas came, Santa Claus brought me a pair of high-top boots to lace up, just like Daddy's, with a neat little knife in a pocket on one side.

"Much better for walking in the rain each day," Mama said.

So I never learned a single thing more except not to leave one drop of pee on the seat in the outhouse. Miss Pollard would leave the room where our thirteen desks were screwed to the floor to inspect the wooden seat with the hole in the middle right after you had gone out to pee and run back in the pouring rain. When she'd come back in, she'd sing out very loud, "Maggie Morrison missed the hole!" to the tune of "The Good Ship Lollipop." Sometimes she would do a little tap or two while she sang. Then I'd have to go back out and wipe up my drip with a piece of Montgomery Ward catalog hanging on a nail in the corner. I'm not going to tell you how she acted when I brought a chopped egg and mayonnaise sandwich for lunch one time. One time.

Frankie was lucky. He still got to take the school bus to the town so he stayed in the same school, but there wasn't any way Mama could sneak me in now that we had moved so much farther away.

Daddy left in February, heading south, and had been gone for nearly three months—who knew where? He hadn't written or sent a word to us, and Mama was out of money.

It was winter. We had big storms. The ocean and beach were on the other side of the highway, and sometimes during a storm the waves washed over the road and filled the ditches. Nights were worse. The wind came whooshing down the small chimney, pushing smoke back into the room. Mama'd send us to bed, then she'd open the front door and flap the back door to let the cold damp wind from off the ocean blow the smoke through the house. Sometimes the storm knocked down power lines and the lights were blown out. Then Mama poked the fire and lit candles. She heated bricks in the oven, wrapped them in newspapers, and put them under the blankets at the foot of our beds. Times when the wind hit the front door, it was like someone was pounding, trying to come in out of the cold. Danny'd be scared and crawl into Mama's lap. I did too. Still, I hoped it was Daddy coming home.

In bed, Danny and me, we watched the rug by the front door ripple into small waves on the linoleum. Danny shivered and snuggled closer.

"Boogie Man! Look, Maggie—Boogie Man!" He'd point at the rippling rug.

"No, no, it's the wind. There's no such things as the Boogie Man."

"Uh-huh. Is too."

I moved the warm brick closer to his feet. When the wind rattled the windows, I wondered. Sometimes I could hear Mama say to Frankie, "Why haven't we heard from him? Where is he? He could be laying dead anywhere, and I would never know it! He could be in China for all I'll ever know! I'm about at my wits' end. . . ." Frankie was always there, keeping Mama company and sleeping on the couch.

* * *

One night in May the Greyhound bus stops in front of our cottage to give Mama the message that her own daddy has died of a heart attack. I see the bus driver put his arms around her and pat her on the back when she cries. The people riding the bus keep gawking out the window and so do Frankie and Danny. Then Mama tells us it's an old friend, Harold Hazelworth, who she used to go to school with in Valley Hill. When we find out it is our only grandpa who died, we all cry our eyes out with our mama.

The next morning, we catch the same bus heading back to Valley Hill so we can be with Grandma. We leave most of what we own behind, which Mama says isn't worth a hill of beans anyhow. "Mostly broken-down beds and a table," she says. "Doesn't matter now. Nothing matters now."

"Hard times," Harold, the bus driver, says when he places our suitcase and two cardboard boxes in the baggage hole on the side of the bus. "And it don't look like it'll get much better any too soon." He smiles, but Mama just shakes her head and gets us on the bus. She doesn't talk all the way so we're quiet too. I don't know about hard times, but the seats are sure soft, and there's lots to see out the window as we go along.

But when we get to Grandma's house in Valley Hill,

the times don't seem so hard to me anymore. In fact, Grandma's house is much bigger and a lot warmer, which is better, except that now we aren't living with Daddy, and Mama has to get a job clerking in Conklin's Emporium and Dry Goods store on Main Street, which is across the street from the Sprouse Reitz I just mentioned—where I steal all my Christmas presents.

After we get to Grandma's house, I worry a lot about my daddy. I believe Daddy is still walking down the highway in the rain, his packsack on his back, heading all the way to the California border, looking for another job. Before he got laid off, he wasn't just a logger, he was the donkey engineer who pulled the logs out of the woods with a big steam engine and heavy cables, then stacked them in big piles for the little steam train, the One Spot, to haul down the mountain.

I ask my mama, "How is Daddy going to know how to find us? How will we know where he is?"

But Mama says he's probably laid up drunk somewhere and has forgotten all about us, and I am to quit pestering her with so many questions this very minute because I'm giving her a headache, and she has more important things on her mind than to listen to my constant chatter.

When I ask her, "What things?" she gives me that

look which means: That's enough out of you, young lady. Stop that right now. So I do.

Two days after Grandpa's funeral—which we don't get to see because Mama says we are too young and that funerals are not for children—I hear her talking to Grandma when she thinks I'm asleep on the rag rug in front of the little gas heater. Mama's crying, saying she can't go through having another one, how is she going to feed the three mouths she already has, not counting her own? And Grandma, who's a Christian Scientist and prays a lot and marks her little books she calls Quarterlies with blue chalk, says don't worry, she'll take her to see Dr. Jones. "You're going to be all right."

A few days later, Grandma is helping Mama walk as they come into the house. Mama's face is white. She says she has the flu and goes right upstairs to bed. She gives me a note and some money and tells me to give it to Mrs. Ziegler—and only Mrs. Ziegler—at Ziegler's grocery store, which said: *2 boxes of Modess wrapped in brown paper.* I didn't ask what that was. She looked too sick. But she was back at work two days later.

But that happened in May when I was still nine, and I didn't steal my Christmas presents until the first day of winter on the shortest day of the year.

Daddy finally finds us, but he doesn't stay for long. One night in the middle of summer when we're all asleep, he comes pounding on Grandma's front door, yelling to open up, he wants to see his kids. Danny and I are sleeping in the front bedroom in the big bed upstairs. We wake up, but Frankie, who is thirteen, is sleeping on the army cot near the brick chimney; he stays asleep. Nobody but Mama can wake Frankie once he shuts his eyes. Which Mama says is because he's a growing boy, the same thing she always says, no matter what he's doing to make me mad.

I open the upstairs window and try to see Daddy, but I can't. The porch light is on, but the porch roof is in the way. Then I hear Mama moan. She sleeps in the back bedroom upstairs, and I hear her feet land on the wood floor, then creep down the narrow stairs. I can barely make out Grandma's voice, but I can tell Daddy is still on the porch, not in the house. Mama hurries back upstairs and begins shaking Frankie, telling him, "Wake up, wake up, and go get the police, hurry!" Frankie, all shaky, gets into his pants and shoes before he's even awake. He stumbles down the stairs and sneaks out the back door to run the back way to the courthouse jail.

Grandma is saying, low and very firm, "Now, Delbert, please, you can't come in, you must go now, you're waking up the whole neighborhood." Then the rumble of Daddy's voice, and again, Grandma's. "Please, Delbert, you're not yourself tonight, why don't you go get some sleep and come back tomorrow?"

I see the police car's headlights coming around the corner and stopping in front of Grandma's house. A big man gets out and comes up the narrow walkway, past the monkeytail tree Grandpa planted when Frankie was born. I see Frankie run from the police car toward the side of the house.

The policeman stops at the bottom of the front steps. "Is that you, Smokey? It's a little late to come calling, wouldn't you say? Come on now, you calm down and let Mrs. Richards get back to sleep, all right? Come with me, we can iron it all out in the morning." I hear his heavy shoes climb the stairs.

It sounds like Daddy is crying when he says, "I just wanted to see my kids, Slim, is that against the law? She stole my kids, Slim."

"You're gonna see your kids, Smokey, but not to-night," the policeman says. "You've had a little too much to drink. You don't want your kids to see you this way. Let's go sleep it off. Good night, Mrs. Richards. I'm sorry about this. He's going to be okay." Then I see them walking to the car, the sheriff with his arm around my daddy's shoulders.

Danny and I watch the big car drive away. "Where's Daddy going? Didn't he come to take us home?"

"No, I think he's going to jail."

"Jail? Did he do something bad?"

"No. He just wanted to see us."

"Maybe that's bad, now that we don't live with him no more."

"It's not bad. He's our daddy. Now get back into bed and go to sleep before Mama comes in."

As soon as they drive off, Frankie comes crawling out from behind the hydrangea bush and sneaks past the lawn and the monkeytail tree and up the steps. When he comes up the stairs Mama calls him, and he goes into her bedroom and closes the door. When he comes out again, the air in our bedroom begins to smell like cigarette smoke. Grandma, who sleeps downstairs, doesn't approve of smoking so Mama usually smokes in her room or the bathroom and blows the smoke out the back window. Tonight she forgets. When Frankie comes back to bed, I can tell by the way he's snuffling that he's been crying.

"Why are you crying?" I ask in a loud whisper.

"Shut up! Don't talk to me." His voice is hoarse.

"Is it because the policeman took Daddy to jail?"

"No, and I said shut up! I'm glad he's going to jail. I

hope they keep him there and never let him out. Now, leave me alone!"

I couldn't believe my ears. "Frankie, you don't mean that."

"The hell I don't! You don't know anything. You don't know what he's done to her. You didn't hear how he talked to her when he was drunk and what he did to her, how he hit her. You were always asleep. He's a mean sonofabitch and if he comes around here again, I'll kill him!"

"Frankie! Don't talk like that—he's your daddy."

"He may be your daddy, but he ain't mine. He told me so one time when he was drunk."

I suck in my breath. "No, Frankie, no, that can't be true—what did Mama say?"

Suddenly Frankie is beside my bed, grabbing me by the shoulders, squeezing hard. His face is close to mine. "Don't you never say a thing about this to my mother, do you hear me? You do and you'll be sorry for the rest of your life." He's crying again, and his voice is cracking high and low. Then he stops hurting me and says, "Please, Maggie, don't say anything to Mama."

I rub my sore shoulders and think about it for a minute; then I say, "Okay, I won't."

"Promise me."

"I promise."

He begins snorting up the snot from all his crying; then he gives me a little shove. "Move over. I'm going to sleep with you and Danny tonight."

"Are you going to wet the bed?"

"No, dammit, you know I don't do that no more."

I hold my ground. "You got to promise."

"Okay, so I promise." He gives me another shove, harder this time. I roll Danny over and move him to the middle of the bed. We both lie down and close our eyes and are quiet for a while. I can tell by the way Frankie is still sniffing that he isn't asleep yet. So I ask him, "When do you think we'll see Daddy again?"

"I don't know. I hope never. Now shut up, I was almost asleep." Then he turns his back, and I lie there looking out the window, where I can see the faint glow of the streetlight on the corner where the big car turned to take Daddy to jail. If Frankie is right, I think, I may never see my daddy again.

* * *

But I do.

It's the day before Labor Day weekend and three days after my tenth birthday. I'm walking down Main Street on my way to the dime store to buy the school supplies I need to start fifth grade in my new school on

Tuesday. All summer I've loved hanging around the five-and-dime, just looking. Even though I never have the money, I like to rattle the paper clips in their boxes and practice pronouncing in a whisper the word "Ti-con-der-oga" while I slowly slide the twelve shiny yellow pencils back and forth in the narrow cardboard band that holds them in two perfect rows of six. I never spill them, not even once. I hold the unsharpened ends up to my nose and smell the pink cedar wood and wonder how they get those black dots of graphite looking like bull's-eyes exactly in the center of the wood pencil. If an ink pad happens to be open I stamp "Fragile" and "Air Mail" on the insides of my arms.

Then I leave the stationery section to see what's new in the toy section. Usually before then Mrs. Wilson, who owns the store, makes me leave. But if my older cousin Patsy, my daddy's niece, is working that day, she just says, "Don't break anything, Maggie, and don't put anything in your pockets."

I say, "I won't." I never do. Not until it's getting to be around Christmas. By then things have changed.

They start to change that day before Labor Day weekend when I'm walking past Clem's Pool Hall and Beer Parlor. I hear a familiar whistle coming from just inside the open door. I walk real slow, trying to see inside the dark parlor whose windows are painted dark green. I can hear the jukebox and the crack of one billiard ball hitting another, but I can't see a thing. And then I hear the whistle again, and I know my daddy is inside calling to me. I stop and wait, afraid to go closer, just in case I'm wrong.

Daddy comes out on the sidewalk and whistles again. "Who's that pretty young lady walking down the street?" He's grinning now.

"Hi, Daddy."

"You got a kiss for your old man?" I nod, and he bends down and puts his arms around me. When he hugs me, his cheek on mine feels smooth as glass. I can smell his shaving lotion and the beer he's been drinking.

"Where have you been?" I ask, hoping he isn't going to tell me he's just got out of jail from the time he'd made that trouble at Grandma's.

"I've been working over by Gales Creek. First time I've been in town since—well, since the last time. How's Danny and Frankie?"

"They're fine."

"And your mother?"

"She's fine."

He's quiet, squinting at the bright blue sky like he's expecting rain. "And you? You're fine. Everybody's fine?"

"Uh-huh."

"Where's your mother?"

"She's working."

"Oh? She's working? Where is she working?"

I motion my head across the street toward the Emporium. "At Conklin's. She's in charge of notions and dry goods." I'm beginning to feel like Daddy and I don't know each other anymore. We don't know what to talk about. After a couple of minutes when we don't say a thing, I say, "I gotta go, Daddy."

"Hold on a minute. Where you headed in such a hurry?"

I tell him about having to buy my school supplies at the Sprouse Reitz five-and-dime, and then I have to get home to keep an eye on Danny while Grandma takes her nap.

"You got plenty of time," he says. "Come on in and have a Coke. I want to give you something."

He takes my hand and leads me through the door. From outside on the sidewalk, the beer parlor looks dark and mysterious, but inside it looks a lot like the other ones I've been in before with Daddy, like the Anchor Inn down on the Newport waterfront, and the one at the Waldport ferry slip where Daddy gave me brass slugs to play the slot machines while he talked to his friends. The same smell—stale beer, cigarette smoke, and dirty socks.

Daddy says for me to meet his two logger friends, Hawkshaw and Cougar Bill. Even though it's still summer, and hot, they're wearing flannel shirts with the arms rolled up. Under their shirts, the dirty sleeves of their union suits hang down to their hairy wrists. Their pants are held up with wide yellow-green suspenders. On their feet they wear scuffed black dress shoes with tiny holes in the toes. Daddy told me one time that a logger will never wear his cork boots to town because the nails on the soles would get worn down from walking on cement sidewalks. "And in the woods, a good pair of cork boots can save your life," he said. I used to unlace his oily black boots when he came home from work at night. I loved the smell he wore then of neat's-foot oil, trees, fresh wood sap, and his sweat.

Daddy's friends smile at me and offer to shake hands, which I do. Daddy laughs. He's wearing a pair of dark blue suit pants and a starched white shirt. A maroon tie is loosened a little below the collar. He wears dark blue suspenders, very narrow, with a thin maroon stripe down the center. His suit coat is hanging on the back of the chair by the pool table. It looks brand new.

He orders me a Coke and himself another beer; then he sticks out his foot. "Want to spit on my new Florsheims?"

I smile and shake my head at the game we used to play.

"Do you need some money?"

"No, I got enough." I open my hand and show him the quarter Mama has given me.

"That's not enough. Here." He puts a five-dollar bill on top of the quarter. I'm rich! "Something for your birthday," he says. "What're you going to buy for school?"

"Two pencils and a Big Five writing tablet."

"Now you can buy an eraser too."

"Thanks, Daddy! I gotta go!"

Daddy laughs again and sips his beer. Before I can leave, Hawkshaw and Cougar Bill slip quarters and dimes and nickels into my pockets. By the time I leave Clem's Pool Hall and Beer Parlor, I jangle with coins. I almost bump into a customer as I rush through the screen door of the five-and-dime.

My cousin Patsy says, "Hey! Slow down, Maggie. You going to a fire?"

"Sorry," I mumble, and hurry to the back, where the pencils and writing tablets and brand-new book bags are stacked. It takes no time for me to gather my school supplies and put them in my new red-plaid rubberized rainproofed book bag. When I've made my choices, I bring the bulging book bag up to Patsy. She unbuckles it and carefully places each item on the counter: a dozen Ticonderoga pencils; a small pencil sharpener, red; two Big Five writing tablets; a full box of paper clips; erasers for pencil and ink; a blue cloth-covered loose-leaf notebook; a package of three-hole notebook paper wrapped in cellophane; a box of paper hole reinforcers; a bottle of blue-black ink and an Esterbrook fountain pen; a large box of Crayolas, which I decide I'll share with Danny after I wear down the tips; and ten red and ten black licorice whips, which I will give one of each to Frankie and Danny after dinner. I also buy Mama a jar of Ponds cold cream, and for Grandma, a small dishtowel.

Patsy looks around to see if Mrs. Wilson is in the store; then she looks me straight in the eye.

"Maggie, these things cost a lot of money."

"I know."

"Do you have the money?"

"Yes."

"Show me."

I dig into my coverall pocket and put the five-dollar bill and all the change on the counter. Patsy's eyes get big. She leans forward and squints at me. "Maggie, where did you get all this money?" She's almost whispering.

"From my daddy. And his friends."

"Uncle Smokey is back?"

"Uh-huh."

"Back where?"

"He's over at Clem's."

"Uh-huh! I see. I didn't know that." She's still staring into my eyes. Then she shakes herself awake. "Well, gee whiz, you sure have got yourself a few school supplies, haven't you? Let's see what it comes to." She begins to list things one by one on her sales pad. She adds it up and smiles. "Four dollars and sixteen cents, Maggie. Looks like you've got plenty of money left over." She takes the five-dollar bill and counts the change, eighty-four cents, into my hand. Then she carefully places my new school supplies in the book bag and hands it to me. I remember to smile and say thanks to Patsy; then I gather up my change and hurry home.

When I come into the kitchen, Grandma is sitting at the oak table finishing a cup of Postum. Danny is beside her drawing a picture of a house with smoke coming out the chimney. I proudly place the bag on the table and carefully spread its treasures in front of them. Before Grandma can ask, I tell her, "Daddy was at Clem's and he gave me some money for my birthday to buy school supplies." Grandma admires everything. When I give her the new dishtowel, she says, "Well, isn't this nice, thank you, dear," and goes into her bedroom to take her nap. I'm so happy I let Danny pick both a red and a black licorice whip to chew on now instead of waiting until after dinner.

When Mama comes home, the frown line between her eyebrows is very deep. She spots my school supplies on the table. She looks shocked and drops into a chair.

"Where did these come from?"

"Maggie bought them," Danny says with black licorice lips.

She glares at me. "You bought them? Where did you get the money?"

"Daddy gave it to her for her birthday," Danny says.

"Your father gave you money? How much money?"

"Five dollars."

"Five dollars? Where is it? Did you spend it all?"

"No, I have some left."

"Give it to me."

I reach into my pocket and place the handful of change on the table. Mama just stares at it. Then she says to Grandma, who is standing over by the sink peeling potatoes, "He came into the store just as we were closing. I could tell right away that he'd been drinking. Luckily there were no customers, but Mr. Conklin was up on the mezzanine. He probably heard every word. He said he could rent a place on the river not too far from the logging camp. I said no, I couldn't take it anymore. He got real mad. He said no wife of his was ever going to work as long as he was head of the family, and he wanted to see the kids. I said not when he was like that, and that I needed money for the kids' school clothes. He just laughed and said, 'You wanted to be on your own, so now you're on your own,' and walked out."

Mama begins to cry. She waves her hand over my school supplies. "But he gives Maggie what? Six or seven dollars? To throw away on all this—this—when I work long hours standing on my feet each day, and only make eleven dollars and fifty cents a week?" She slaps the table. The coins bounce. "Well, that's it. I need a lawyer." She holds her head in her hands.

Grandma sighs and runs water into the pan of potatoes. "Bill Hadley's son just opened up his law office above the bank. You could go see him, I suppose." She places the pan on a back burner and scratches a match on the matchbox hanging on the wall behind the stove. She turns on the gas and touches the match to the burner.

I stare into the blue and pink flame under the pot until it begins to change shape and color. I don't know how long before Mama pokes me with her finger, hard.

"Stop staring like that! Put this stuff away and set the table."

✳ ✳ ✳

Just before Christmas we're having recess in the school basement because we can't go outside, it's always raining. Another cousin, Patsy's little sister, Dottie Mae, comes over and stands beside me while I wait my turn to practice ball bouncing on the cement floor. She taps me on the shoulder and says in a shy voice, "I heard about Uncle Smokey, Maggie."

I turn. "What? What did you hear?"

"Well, you know—"

"Know what?"

"That he's in jail. Didn't you know he's in jail?"

I clench my fists, and Dottie Mae steps back. She knows firsthand about the bad temper I've grown lately. She was there when I knocked out Johnny Baker's front tooth in the school yard after the first day of school. "He is not!"

"My mama said he is."

I move closer so no one else can hear. When her back is against the cold cement wall, I say, "How come she knows anything?"

"Her friend Maude at the courthouse said so. She told Mama that Uncle Smokey, he beat up the deputy who gave him the papers for divorce, and he's gotta stay in jail for a long, long time."

"That's a lie! You just shut your mouth! You better watch out what you say!"

I decide not to say a word to Mama, but she already knows. She tells Frankie and me that night. "I'm sorry he's in jail, but he brought it on himself. It's not my fault he hit a policeman. You and Maggie go see him tomorrow. See if he will give you some money. It's almost Christmas—you kids need shoes, and he is still your father."

"Not me—I'm not going," Frankie says.

"Frankie! Stop that—you're going! Maggie is not going to that jail alone."

* * *

Saturday it's raining steady as we walk to the county courthouse and go down the steps to the basement door with the sign on the glass window that reads: County Jail.

Frankie stops on the bottom step. "I'm not gonna ask him for money, so you can forget that!"

"We *can't* forget that. Look at your shoes. You're wearing those old tennis shoes in the rain, and they've got holes! You need heavy shoes for the winter, and you know it. Frankie, Mama needs us to help her."

"Okay, then, but you have to be the one to ask him, not me. I'm not going to ask him for a single thing as long as I live."

"Okay, I will. But you gotta act nice."

He pushes open the big door. We step into a room with benches, a counter to one side, and a desk against a gray cement wall. Otherwise, the room is empty. No prison cells like in the movies. No convict in a black-and-white-striped suit dragging a ball and chain, no prison guard to frisk us before we see the prisoner. No rubber hose, no big light for the third degree. Frankie and I look at each other.

"There's nobody here," I whisper. "Maybe the jail is empty."

"Yeah, let's get out of here quick." Frankie turns to leave.

I jump when suddenly I hear someone laughing. It's coming from down a narrow corridor. And it sounds like Daddy. We slip over to where we can take a peek and see the rows of iron bars lining both sides of the hall. At the open door of the last cell, there sits our daddy on a stool, talking to the big policeman, Slim. We don't know what to do. We just stand there until Daddy notices us.

"Well, look who's here. Come on down here and let's have a look at you. What a wonderful surprise!"

Daddy walks out to meet us. He hugs and kisses us. "Didn't I tell you I have great kids, Slim?"

"You sure did, Smoke, and I'm glad they came to see you, but you better get on back inside just in case someone else comes in. You haven't seen the judge yet."

Daddy takes my hand and leads me into his cell. He motions us to the cot against one wall. Frankie lags behind. "Sit down, kids, make yourself comfortable," he says, but now Daddy doesn't look too comfortable himself. He puckers his lips, makes little whistling sounds, and looks around at the dirty cement walls. Sweat pops out on his forehead. He swipes his hand across his face and back over his head. I notice he's getting balder. The skin on his head shines in the overhead light. Frankie sits on the edge of the cot near the open door and stares at his wet sneakers. His long black hair hangs down in front, hiding his face.

Daddy keeps his hand over his mouth, even when he's talking, but I can tell by the way his eyes squint that he's smiling at me. "It's so good to see you. You're getting to be quite a young lady." I blush, hoping he isn't noticing the two bumps that are growing on my chest under Frankie's big old sweatshirt.

"It's almost Christmas," he says. "What do you want Santa to bring you?"

I shrug. I'm tongue-tied.

Frankie sits hunched, looking out through the bars. Daddy nudges Frankie's sneaker with his shoe. I notice that the new black Florsheims he was so proud of on Labor Day are scuffed, no longer shiny. "Hey, aren't you talking to your old man? Don't you know how to say hello?"

" 'Lo," Frankie mutters, without a crack in his voice.

"Stand up and look at me when I talk to you, young man. I taught you better manners than that."

Frankie stands up fast, looking around the cell and at Daddy's shoes. Everywhere but into Daddy's face.

". . . and it looks like you could use a decent haircut." It used to be something Daddy did for us, give us a haircut or take us to the barber.

Frankie turns and walks to the cell door, then faces Daddy. "I don't have to listen to you anymore. I hate you. I'm glad you're here. I hope they throw away the key! Come on, Maggie, let's get out of here." He begins to run down the corridor.

"Frankie, no!" I start to follow.

Daddy grabs my arm. "Maggie, wait!"

I try to pull away. I'm crying. "I gotta go with Frankie."

Daddy holds me by the shoulders. His hands shake. His eyes are wet. "Maggie, look, I'm sorry you have to see your old man this way. I know it's not right. I'll make it up to you somehow. Don't hate your daddy. You're my little girl. Look, look, wait, I want to give you something." He steps to the cell door and calls, "Slim, hey, Slim, give Maggie all the money I had on me when you brought me in, all right? I just cashed my paycheck last weekend, it was two months' pay. Give it to her, Slim. It's Christmas."

Daddy kisses me on the cheek. He's trying to smile at me without showing his teeth, but I see where one of his big front teeth is broken off at the root. It makes him look ugly. My daddy's handsome face is gone. His whole face has changed into one I don't know.

"Go see Slim. Go ahead." He gives me a little pat and a push. In a daze, I walk back down the narrow corridor past empty cells.

Slim is standing behind the counter, holding a large envelope. "I'm sorry, little lady, but your dad was broke when our deputies brought him in. He just don't remember. He's a good man, your dad, but he's got himself a little problem which is getting him into some trouble. He's probably going to be here for a while, so you and your brother come see him again. All right?"

I keep my eyes on my shoes, cold and wet from the long walk in the rain. Then I nod yes. But I know I'm lying. I'm not coming back. No matter how long—I'm not coming back.

And then I go to the dime store and steal all my Christmas presents.

For my mother I steal a set of carved wooden bookends of sleeping Mexicans wearing huge sombreros; for Grandma, a pair of glass salt and pepper shakers with shiny silvery tops; for Danny, six little khaki-colored rubber soldiers carrying rifles; and for Frankie, I steal a pair of thick gray socks to keep his feet warm and dry in his sneakers. I walk out of the store with my presents stuffed in my pockets and under Frankie's sweatshirt. No one sees me. It's Christmastime. Mrs. Wilson and my cousin Patsy are too busy to notice.

I creep into Grandma's closet under the stairs. Hanging on the back of the door is her soft flannel nightgown, and next to it, Grandpa's striped flannel nightshirt she'd sewed for him, which still smells of the pink peppermints he loved. I wrap myself in the soft, worn flannel, crying, breathing in my grandpa, my grandma, two people I know really loved me. I feel like I never want to leave this closet where Grandpa's gray business suits used to hang and where Grandma still keeps her church dresses and black wool coat. Part of me is surprised when I look at the presents I've stolen—did I really do that? Another part knows I'm going to get punished for what I did.

I leave the door open for just enough light to wrap

my presents in Grandma's white tissue paper. I hide them in back of the tree under the lowest branches. Two nights later, on Christmas Eve, we open our presents, and everyone opens mine.

This time, no one asks me where I got the money.

The Art Lesson

She ain't my aunt, she says, not really. Just because she's married to my uncle Lester don't make her no aunt. So she says for me not to call her Aunt Ramona, okay? Besides, she says, who knows how long she's going to be *anybody's* aunt by the way things are going around here, so just to call her Ramona, she says, okay?

"I mean, you call this a real marriage?" she says. "Living with a holier-than-thou mother-in-law in this run-down house, with a man who thinks he's God's gift to women, and me left here to take care of a squalling, red-faced brat all day? You call this *living*?"

She looks at me like I'm suppose to know if all those things she says is a *living*, but what do I know? I'm just a ten-year-old kid. I look around Grandma's kitchen, seeing if I can come up with some kind of answer that'll make Aunt Ramona—Ramona—feel friendly toward me, and still stay a part of my family, which she seems to think stinks. Me and my mother, and my two brothers, we just moved here from the coast a month ago. We were living with Grandma till last week when Mama rented us our own old house down the street a block. So I don't really know Ramona that much.

Her and her baby Sweet Pea, or Pea Pea—that's what they call him—they've been up there visiting her mother and two sisters in Ketchikan, Alaska, for most of the time we've been at Grandma's, so how could I know her? She just came back five days ago. This is the first time I've come to Grandma's house when she wasn't home, so I've never been alone before with Aunt Ramona—I mean, Ramona.

"Well, kid," she says. "Cat got your tongue, or what?"

She stands there with her hands on her hips looking down at me, her frizzy red hair as tangled as a bird's nest, tied back by a wide pink satin ribbon with a bow sticking up on top. She's wearing a tight bright kelly green sweater which pokes her out in front pretty much, and her slacks are a dark maroon. She has on this dark red lipstick with a little bow shape painted perfect on her top lip. Her eyebrows are black and about as thin as they can get and still have something growing out of

her skin. I know this means she plucks them with
tweezers. Mama does the same thing hunched over a
mirror, so I know it's something ladies do to make
themselves beautiful, but it sure isn't something I'll ever
try, never mind that I don't have two eyebrows, but
practically only this one that runs all the way across my
forehead.

"Where's Grandma?" I ask Aunt Ramona—I mean,
Ramona.

"It's Wednesday. She's gone to her church to read
her Bible. She couldn't read right here and watch her
grandchild once in a while, but, no, she gets her hat on
and goes to church. It takes all kinds."

I look in the office, which used to be the front room.
"Where's Uncle Lester?"

"Your good-lookin' good-for-nothin' uncle's uptown.
So whaddya want?"

She sits herself down at the big oak table covered
with Grandma's oilcloth with the red strawberries
painted on it that I like, and pushes the vinegar and oil
cruets and the Heinz ketchup bottle to the side. She
pulls some typing paper in front of her and picks up
a pencil. She has the morning *Oregonian* folded to
the funny pages, and then I see she has a drawing of
Maggie and Jiggs almost finished on the paper in front
of her.

"Gee, that's good, Aunt Ramona—I mean, Ramona," I say. "I didn't know you could draw."

"I can't. Who says I can? This here stinks."

"No, it doesn't. It looks just like them."

There's Maggie, tall and skinny and red-haired, holding a rolling pin over her head, and there's Jiggs. He's sneaking out in his stocking feet carrying a bucket, which I know from reading the funnies he's going to get filled with suds, which is a funny way to get beer since my daddy used to get his in brown quart bottles after hours from Dave, the bootlegger, or he made it himself in a crock behind the stove.

"What do you know?" she says. "You're just a dumb scabby-kneed little kid." But she says this with a smile that shows all her teeth. So I smile back and don't talk, even though I want to tell her she's got a smear of red lipstick on the two front ones that kind of buck out a little over the top of her lower lip. She hunches over her drawing, and I sit down in the chair next to her. She tells me to sit on the other side so's I don't accidentally bump her left elbow and make her make a mistake, and then I know it's okay for me to be there watching her finish her drawing. I also notice now that she is left-handed like me, which I know means something, but I don't know what. So I move to the other side and don't say a word, just hold my breath. The way she puts the eyelashes on Maggie and draws the polka dot circles on her skirt is just perfect. Then the baby—that's Sweet Pea—begins to howl, and she throws the pencil down.

"Another county heard from," she says, and goes into the back room. I hear her holler, "Shut up, you little brat!" and "Hey, you! Kid! Bring me that baby bottle on the drainboard."

I fetch the baby bottle and take it in to her. Sweet Pea's face is beet red, and his little body is stiff and shaking, but she jams the rubber nipple in his mouth, and he quits his howling and starts sucking away. She props the bottle on a pillow and walks out. I stand there for a minute by the little wicker basket on legs, looking down at this baby, trying to see if I like him or not. I don't know him at all, but he is my cousin so I figure I should feel some kind of love for him now that he's part of my family. But I just don't. I'm not going to tell his mama, Aunt Ramona—Ramona—what I think, which is that he's scrawny and ugly, with his big red nose and those little white pimples all over his cheeks. I hope she doesn't ask me. He doesn't look anything like my uncle Lester, who is very handsome, and he sure doesn't look like Aunt Ramona—I mean, Ramona—who I decide looks just like a real movie star, don't ask me which.

"Hey, kid! You better get yourself out of there before he starts in again," she yells.

I say, "Okay." I've seen enough to last me a long time. "Ugly as a mud fence," my mama'd say, if she took the time. One look and you'd have to say it—he's a real ugly little kid. Aunt Ramona-Ramona is a lot more interesting.

There's a big jar of water and a little black box of watercolors on the table now. She's grinding a tiny wet brush in one of the color squares. She shapes the brush into a point very carefully before she puts red stripes on Jiggs's socks. I see she's got red paint on her fingers now. I worry she'll get it on the drawing, but she just reaches over and grabs a diaper off the old high chair Grandma has kept in her kitchen since we were all babies. The diaper gets a few red smears before she puts it in her lap. She leans over the drawing again and paints one, two, then three red stripes. She hasn't gone outside the lines, not even once. "So where's your old man?" she asks, just like that.

I keep my eyes on the brush. "I don't know."

She swirls the brush in the jar of water and says, "What happened to him?"

"I don't know," I say again, and watch the water turn strawberry pink.

She jams the brush in the orange square and starts grinding away, making a puddle of soapy orange paint, straightens out the bristles, wipes her hand off, and asks, "How come you ran off and left him?"

I'm busy watching how Maggie's hair turns bright orange under the brush, so I don't answer.

"Well?"

"I don't know. Mama said we had to."

She lets out a snort. "I bet it was the booze. I bet he got mean. They're all alike."

She swishes the brush in the water again and starts soaking it with black paint. Her head is low over her paper, and her frizzy hair is in the way so I have to move back some to see how she's filling in Jiggs's black pants, bringing the tip of the brush right up to the pencil line every single time. I know now I'm watching a real artist, just like Goofy but different.

She's still talking. "You give 'em the best years of your life, not to mention how they're the ones who knock you up in the first place, and then they act like they're doing you a big favor marrying you. Like they're the innocent party and you got yourself that way all by yourself. Your mom's lucky she got out when she did. Better late than never, that's for sure. If she'd been smart she woulda quit after the first kid, instead of getting herself tied down with two more squalling brats." It looks like she's saying all this to Jiggs, but I know she means me and Danny.

I keep my eyes on the brush. Jiggs's trousers are finished, all shiny wet and black. I'm trying not to hear what Aunt Ramona-Ramona is saying about my mama, trying to imagine how it would've been if she'd only had Frankie, but I can't. I'm already here, and so is Danny. But I wonder, would it be easier on Mama now that we don't live with Daddy anymore if she'd done what Aunt Ramona-Ramona said, have only one kid? But then, where would I be now? I get a big hollow feeling in my stomach like I'm hungry, and keep my eyes on the brush. Maggie's high-heeled shoes now have little white dots on the pointed toes. It makes them look like they are made of brand-new patent leather sparkling in the sun.

"Listen, kid, let me give you a little piece of advice for free, no charge. Don't get married and don't have kids. Do something with your life besides wiping snotty noses and dirty behinds and waiting on your lord and master hand and foot. If someone told me what I'm telling you, I wouldn't be here right now—I can tell you that's for sure."

She looks right at me for a second, then aims the

brush like a dart and tosses it in the jar of water. She just sits there for a minute looking at her chipped nail polish before she starts peeling it off in little strips of red paint. I see she hasn't finished the painting of Maggie and Jiggs, but I don't say anything because she looks like she's through talking for a while and is just going to sit there and think. It isn't as if she forgot I'm there—she knows I'm there, all right.

So I try to do some thinking too about all the stuff she's saying. But I don't know anything. Nobody tells me what's going on. All I know is that we were living at Grandma's until Mama couldn't stand living in the same house with Uncle Lester after he moved in with his wife and baby. That's why we're living in this old house a block down the street where mice or rats run up and down inside the walls at night.

"She's going to get a divorce, isn't she?" Aunt Ramona-Ramona says.

"Divorce?"

"Yeah, you've heard of divorce. It means they're going to split up, get unhitched, untie the knot, dump the old ball and chain. You know, call it quits."

"I don't know," I say, and I decide right then and there that I never ever want to have to say I don't know to nobody ever again because of how it makes me feel, not just dumb, but like I got no say in what happens to me. Like somebody else gets to be the boss of my life all the time.

I look at the funny papers in front of us on the table. Maggie's holding that rolling pin over her head like she's going to bonk Jiggs. I know that Maggie probably never felt the way I feel right now, having to keep saying I don't know to Aunt Ramona-Ramona.

"It's okay for her," Aunt Ramona-Ramona says. "It ain't against her religion. Me, I get a divorce, I go straight to Hell, know what I mean?"

I don't know the answer to that question either. I don't know about hell except that it's a swear word, so I just keep quiet and look at the cartoon Maggie and that rolling pin. My name is Maggie too, but I don't connect myself with this Maggie in the funny papers who's tall and skinny and has red hair, because I'm short for being ten years old and have straight brown hair and big square front teeth, now that they've finally come in. And this one long eyebrow I already mentioned. The Maggie in the funnies looks more like Aunt Ramona-Ramona, but Jiggs in his striped socks don't look nothin' like my uncle Lester. Uncle Lester never has to take off his shoes and sneak in or out of anywhere. He does whatever he wants whenever he wants, and goes wherever he wants. My uncle has always been more of a stomper than a sneak.

I keep waiting for Aunt Ramona-Ramona to finish peeling her nails so's she'll get back to the painting, which is beginning to look a little dull now that it's drying out. She's still got Maggie's thumb and three fingers to go. It looks like she's not in any hurry now. I don't mind just sitting there beside her, listening to her talk, even if my stomach feels a little bit upside down, because I like the way she smells, like a combination of Juicy Fruit and those teeny tiny black squares she pops in her mouth she calls Sen Sen.

She says, "Up in Alaska people live life a lot different. The women up there, they don't take nothin' off nobody. There's always plenty of work in the cannery, and I got sisters there who don't mind another brat along with all the other brats they already got. Both of them just quit worrying about going to church anymore, they don't bother with divorce neither. They decide they don't like the guy, they just kick him out and get another one that's better. There's a lot more men up there than women, so you can afford to be choosy."

She pushes all those little strips of nail polish into a pile and shoves her painting aside. She looks at me now like she really sees me, and I notice her eyes are a sort of light green.

She says, "What the hell. It's a free country, right?"

I nod yes, but I want her to see that she hasn't finished the painting yet. Jiggs's hair and suspenders and Maggie's rolling pin are still white. She pushes her chair away from the table. I get a little worried.

"Aren't you going to finish it?" I ask.

"Finish what?"

"His suspenders and her rolling pin and her fingers?"

She stands and stretches her long arms above her head. I see some black-and-blue marks inside her upper arm that are beginning to turn yellow and pink, like she must've hurt herself somehow.

"No," she says, "I'm tired of fooling around."

"What are you going to do with it?"

"I'll probably just burn it like all the rest."

I can't believe it! I look into her face to see if she means it.

She asks, "Why? What difference is it to you?"

"I don't think you should do that."

"Oh?" she says, smiling a tiny smile. "Why not?"

"I like it," I say.

"No, you don't."

"I do too, I really like it."

"Why? How come you like it?"

"I think it's good. You're a real artist, Aunt Ramona—I mean, Ramona . . ."

She grins at me, then holds the painting up and fans it in the air. "Well, if you like it, you can have it, if you're *sure* you want it."

"I want it," I say.

"Well, then, kid, it's yours. I'll give it to you as a souvenir. Something to remember me by. How's that?"

She laughs and shows all her teeth again, and the lipstick is still there on the two big front ones, but I'm so happy that she likes me and wants me to have her painting that I don't say a single word. She pushes the paint box toward me and takes the jar of muddied water to the sink and comes back with it full of clear water.

"Here," she says. "Go to it. You finish it. I got some things I gotta do."

I take the brush and slosh it around on the hard square, doing it just the same way she did. I bend over the painting and begin to give Jiggs his yellow hair. I get so busy painting and being careful to stay inside the lines, and not smear the wet places, that I don't pay any attention to what she's doing in the other room. I hear her singing as she slams dresser drawers, which I can't believe doesn't wake up little old Pea Pea, but I don't hear a peep out of him.

I've just finished painting Jiggs's suspenders red when she comes back into the kitchen holding her baby on her hip wrapped in a blanket. She has a suitcase in her other hand. She's wearing that white wool jacket with the bright red and blue and yellow Indian arrow designs on it—the one she got in Alaska—and she's combed her hair and tied on a kelly green ribbon to match her sweater and her eyes.

"Well, kid, I'm off," she says.

"Where you going?"

"Ask me no questions, I'll tell you no lies." She laughs. "But I'm gonna give you one more little piece of free advice. So you listen good now—I ain't gonna repeat it again, okay? You listening?"

I nod and wait.

She touches her long fingernail to my nose and taps it gently. "Don't ever sell your soul for no pickle," she says. "You got that?"

I nod my head yes.

"And don't you ever forget it."

I say I won't forget.

Then she grins again, and I see she's wiped the lipstick off her teeth, and her eyes have those shiny white lights in them like on the toes of Maggie's shoes, and she looks like the most beautiful movie star I've ever seen.

Only more so.

Anchors Away

I hate Mildred Conklin's guts. My best friend Buddy Riley is the only one who knows it, but not even Buddy knows why. And I have a reason—a very good reason. In fact, I have *two* good reasons: the dress, and Mildred's big mouth.

One night after work my mom ducks into the pantry in the garage, which my grandma calls her cellar, to sneak a few drags off a cigarette, and finds the dress stuffed behind the pickle crock with its skirt half ripped clean off the bodice. She comes into the kitchen demanding to know why anyone would do a terrible thing like that to such a nice school dress, especially when dresses like that cost a pretty penny. And she's looking straight at me.

I don't lie. I tell the truth. I did it, I say, and I don't care! I will never, never, ever wear another one of Mildred Conklin's hand-me-downs, no matter what she, my mom, does to me. She can beat me over the head with a baseball bat, she can make me do dishes for a year. I don't care how nice it is, or how much it costs, I am not going to wear another single hand-me-down *anything*, especially one that belonged to that fat slob Mildred Conklin, my mom's boss's daughter!

My mother sits down at the kitchen table and shakes her head. "Don't be silly. No one's going to beat you, for heaven's sake. Why do you always have to exaggerate everything? And you know this dress is practically new. Mildred outgrows things so fast."

"It's not my fault she's so fat," I say.

Mom looks out the window at the double row of zinnias growing beside Grandma's driveway. Without thinking, she reaches inside her jacket pocket and brings out her package of cigarettes and, still looking out the window, lights a Chesterfield. She sighs as the smoke escapes from her mouth. Grandma looks away. I know she doesn't approve of Mom's bad habit, but she doesn't say a word, just takes the dress in her two hands and examines the damage, which is great—I made sure of that. Mom takes another long drag on her cigarette and sighs again. She knocks an ash into the saucer of her coffee cup, and when Grandma notices, she gives her mother a guilty look. "She can't help it either, Maggie. She only wants to be your friend."

I say, "Mom, she's no friend! She waits until everybody is at recess, then she starts saying things like how much she likes my dress, and how good it looks on me, and how it used to be her dress, but she didn't need it anymore, so she had her daddy give it to you to give to me so I'd have something nice to wear to school!" My hands are slapping hard at my cheeks, angry at the tears pouring down.

My mother slips off her shoes and rubs her swollen feet. Eight hours a day standing behind the notions counter in Conklin's Emporium leaves her sore and weary. Her varicose veins look like clusters of blue grapes hanging on the backs of her calves. She massages them as if that could make them disappear.

"Well, don't say any more about it. Just try to be nice to her. That's all I'm asking," Mom says.

Grandma folds the torn dress and ties it into a neat bundle with the sash. "Never mind, it won't go to waste. It'll make good quilting material. I'll start cutting it up in the morning."

"It's a perfectly good dress," my mother protests. "The skirt just needs to be gathered and mended at the waist. Someone can still get some good use out of it."

I start to say, "Not me—" but Grandma interrupts.

"Maggie and I will cut it up in the morning," she

says, giving her daughter a quieting look. My mother dips the tip of her burning cigarette into the black coffee. I hear it sizzle. She lays the soggy butt on the saucer and looks out at the zinnias for a long moment, then gives Grandma a small nod before she stands to go upstairs to change her clothes. We've moved back in with Grandma for a while and my uncle Lester is still living with Grandma too. He does the insurance business since Grandpa died, and is divorced now from Sweet Pea's mama, who used to be my aunt Ramona. We've lived in Valley Hill for almost two years, but it seems a lot longer. I don't know where my daddy is but I know he's not in jail or my mom or my nosy cousin Dottie Mae would tell me.

This Saturday morning I sit in the kitchen with Grandma listening to the snappy sound of Uncle Lester's new Smith-Corona typewriter—easy down payment, two years to pay—clacking away in the living room, which was Grandpa's insurance office and is Lester's office now. Even with the French doors closed between the two rooms—the office and the dining room converted into Grandma's sitting room—I can hear him talking on the phone. Then the receiver slams down hard, and Uncle Lester stomps into the kitchen, his handsome face dark as a thundercloud. He's swearing a blue streak.

"Lester, please," Grandma says, looking up from cutting small squares of cloth out of Mildred's dress. "Mind your language. What's the matter?"

"It's Milt Conklin! He just bought himself a new La Salle. That baby can do a hundred and twenty if it can do a mile." He pours himself a cup of coffee and glares at Grandma. "He's gotta be making damn good dough in that store if he can afford a car like that, let alone pay cold hard cash for the damn thing!"

Lester's shiny new '37 Ford is parked at the curb in front of the house. It has plenty of bright chrome and plenty of speed, but it is no new La Salle. And Lester will be making car payments every month for the next four years. "A little down on a big bill" the newspaper ad read, showing a picture of a large goose.

Grandma says, "Lester, I told you to watch your language in front of Maggie. And you shouldn't talk about one of your customers like that."

"Like what? Huh? What did I say? I didn't say nothin'." He gives her a dumb look and winks at me.

I duck my head so Grandma doesn't see me smile. But I'm so happy! Uncle Lester hates Mildred's father, just like I hate Mildred! I feel his fist hit my shoulder in a hard poke.

"Saw your girlfriend Mildred at the post office," he says.

I slug him back. "Cut it out! She's not my girl-friend."

He laughs. "Boy, the way she's packing it on, she's built like a brick outhouse!"

"Lester! Stop it now! That's enough!" Grandma raises her voice and shakes her scissors at him.

"What? You mean what I said about the brick out-house?"

"You heard me, now—there are children present."

But I have already run outside, swallowing my gig-gles until I'm safely hidden behind the hydrangea bush beside the back steps. There I explode and convulse with joy. *Mildred is a brick outhouse! Outhouse! Out-house!* I'm doubled over. Tears run down my face. My ribs ache from laughing so hard. At that moment I fall in love with my uncle Lester.

"What children?" I hear Uncle Lester say. "I don't see no children."

A few moments later Grandma sticks her head around the hydrangea bush. "What's so funny?" she asks.

"Oh, nothin'," I say, feeling weak and trying to catch my breath.

I know Grandma, who is sweet and kind and goes to the Christian Science Reading Room every Wednesday afternoon and on Sunday to her church, where they teach that God is Supreme Intelligence, God is Truth, God is Love—she wouldn't understand my hate for Mildred, or my love for my uncle, who shares that hate. Grandma never has a bad word to say about anyone except President Roosevelt, who's a Democrat. And even then she never really says anything against him. You just know by the way her mouth puckers up funny when his name is mentioned.

I love my grandma and admire her. She has all her own teeth and both her tonsils. She knits sweaters and crochets granny afghans and tats lace. And she holds quilting parties in her big private room behind the kitchen, which is also her bedroom. There the church ladies sit around a large wooden frame, stitching and talking and eating Grandma's Ambrosia Delight and sticky maple bars from the Dawn bakery. In summer Grandma cans every kind of fruit and vegetable grown in Tualatin Valley and puts up pickle relishes and jams while she listens to Myrt and Marge, Vic and Sade, Easy Aces, and Ma Perkins on the radio. Often I help to put the slippery fruit into glass jars and screw the lids on. One time, I pretended I had a bad stomachache so I could stay home from school to listen to her soap operas with her.

Grandma is still standing on the steps, smiling.

"Would you like to walk uptown with me? I have to get more yarn."

Going uptown, which is only two blocks away, means going into Conklin's store, where I might meet Mildred, or her father, who now, because of Uncle Lester, I also hate. But because Grandma never asks for much, I say, "Okay, Grandma," and run to get my new sailor hat.

The bunions on Grandma's feet make walking slow. The soft black leather of her Red Cross shoes stretches over bulges big as plums. Her two big toes poke painfully away from each other. I shift my feet and try to match Grandma's short steps. She takes my hand in one of her white rayon-gloved ones. She is wearing her navy blue straw hat with the short black veil. Her hair is as white as my sailor hat, which sits squarely on my forehead, two fingers above my eyebrows. In my head I hear a military marching band playing my favorite music, "Anchors Aweigh." I imagine the Stars and Stripes snapping briskly in the breeze. Five hundred able-bodied seamen stand at attention across the street in front of the Methodist church. As we pass in review, Grandma's double chin jiggles smartly in time to the music. I give a practice salute toward my reflection in the window of the Greyhound Bus depot, then tug on my shrunken, stained sweatshirt, getting ready for the next inspection I know will take place as soon as we enter Conklin's store.

My mom looks up from her place at the front counter, where she's pricing spools of grosgrain and taffeta ribbons. Surprised, she smiles, then frowns.

"Oh, Maggie! Why did you wear that old sweatshirt in here? And look at the knees in those pants! Have you been playing in the dirt?"

"We just came uptown to get some yarn," Grandma says. "We won't be very long, Jean."

Mom gives a short, nervous laugh and removes my sailor hat. She spits on her fingers and brushes at the stubborn cowlick that springs out over my forehead. Then she pulls a length of red taffeta ribbon from its spool.

"Wouldn't you like a yard of this for a pretty bow? You're never going to get that cowlick trained unless you tie it back."

"No," I say, and rescue my sailor hat. Before I can escape upstairs with Grandma, Mama grabs the bottom of my sweatshirt and gives a tug, but it's old and it's shrunk, and it leaps back into place, leaving an inch of my belly showing above my belt.

"Oh, well," she sighs. "I keep trying. I don't know why." Her fingers are busy rearranging the pencils beside her sales book when her boss, Mr. Conklin, appears.

"Good morning, Mrs. Richards," he says politely to Grandma; then, noticing me, he smiles and gives me a friendly pat on the shoulder. I feel his hand slide down my back and rub a small circle just below my waist before I step away. He says to my mom, "Aren't our girls growing up, Jean? Maggie, Mildred is around somewhere. Why don't you go find her?"

"Excuse me, Mr. Conklin," Grandma says, "Maggie is going to help me pick out some yarn. We'll go on up to the mezzanine," she tells my mom. "Good day, Mr. Conklin."

I look at my mother, hurrying to put away the rolls of ribbon and rush downstairs to help a twelve-year-old boy haul boxes up to the notions counter. I want to give her a hug, but I've been told never to do that in the store. Someone, especially her boss, Mr. Conklin, might see. She says, "I could lose my job. Then what would we do?"

But Mr. Conklin has moved down the aisle toward women's corsets. My mother pauses and motions that she wants to tell me something.

"What?"

"Come back when you finish with Grandma. I want to buy you something."

"What?"

"Not now, I have to go. Just come back." Then she hurries toward the basement stairs.

Grandma is already at the foot of the creaky wooden stairs to the mezzanine. She clutches the banister and slowly climbs to where Mrs. Hubbard has her knitting department. Mrs. Hubbard is tall and skinny and wears a bony corset that shines pink through her maroon hand-knit bouclé dress. She greets Grandma with a yellow long-toothed smile. I hang back behind the pillar, hoping she doesn't see me. If Mrs. Hubbard asks about my own knitting project, I will have to confess that I ripped out the sleeveless sweater I've been struggling to make as a birthday present for Danny. The mangled mess of yarn is stuffed into a shoe box, which is now hiding under my bed.

But Mrs. Hubbard and Grandma are busy fondling the skeins of wool yarn and holding several different colors up to the dim light. I wander over to the mezzanine railing and look down onto the first floor. I can see my mother putting a stack of boxes on the counter. A customer is waiting for her. There are customers in other departments too, browsing or buying from the other clerk, or being greeted by Mr. Conklin. None of it is very interesting, except for what I can see just below me—the ladies' dressing room. In it, Mrs. Johansen, who owns the ice cream store, is trying on a spring coat. I watch her stuff herself into the light blue shantung and tug on the rhinestone buttons to see if they are sewed on with strong thread. Then she buttons the coat and turns to look at her wide behind in the mirror. She nods to herself and takes off the coat. Mr. Conklin, a sales book in his hand, is waiting for her when she comes out of the dressing room.

When I spot Mildred looking at the dresses in the children's department, I turn my back and duck down behind the railing. The last person I want to see today, or on any other day, especially when she's trying on clothes, is *the brick outhouse, Mildred!* I close my eyes and feel myself shudder. Ugh!

Someone taps me on the shoulder. I jump. It's Grandma.

"Why don't you go down and see what your mama wants, dear. I'm going to be here for a while."

I say, "Okay, Grandma." But it isn't okay. How am I going to get down the stairs and over to my mom's counter without Mildred seeing me? Mildred is so stupid she doesn't even know how much I hate her. Like I say, that isn't something you go around telling someone if your mother works for her father. Through the railing I watch Mildred take a dress and go into the ladies' dressing room. Oh, no, I'm not going to stay here and watch, it's too disgusting! I hurry down the stairs. My mother sees me coming.

"Hurry up! I don't have much time."

"Whatcha gonna buy me?" I have my eye on a white middy blouse with a navy blue tie, but that is too much to hope for. Only last week Mom let me buy my sailor hat just like Buddy's so that we can play Navy. It's too soon to ask for the rest of the uniform. I know money doesn't grow on trees. She doesn't have to keep telling me that.

"Let's go over to Lingerie," she says.

I try out the word. "Lawn-jer-ay." So that's how you pronounce it. When I read the word mounted on the wall over the counter, it sounds more like the "linger" in "lingering." I've never said it out loud before.

"Why are we going to lawn-jer-ay?"

"You'll see." She walks me past the counter displaying pink-and-white bloomers and peach-colored snuggies, the old-lady styles of underpants my grandma and my mama wear. She passes the display of white cotton briefs, my style, and stops at a small table in the middle of the aisle where a group of stacked boxes are marked 30 ABC, 32 ABC, 34 ABC, 36 ABC. Mom opens a lid.

"What color do you want? Pink, peach, or white?"

I see what is stacked in the box. "Oh, no!" I start to leave. She grabs me by the wrist.

"Hold still!"

"No!"

She shakes my arm and keeps her voice low. "Be sensible! You're developing too fast. You need to wear a bra."

"No, Mama, please—"

She says in a loud whisper, "I said you are growing up. You're not a little girl anymore, Maggie. Now stand still. I've got to measure you. Please do not make a fuss." She reaches in her pocket and brings out a tape measure.

I hold my arms away from my sides while she wraps the tape around my chest. I feel it pressing against my two hard round bumps. It's hurting me. I begin to squirm. The tape slips. My mother grabs again at my wrist and gives it a quick shake. She's too mad to see Mr. Conklin standing beside her.

"Time to buy the young lady a bra, Jean? What size does she take?"

"I don't know. The tape slipped—I mean—"

"Well, let me see," he says, and clamps his hand firmly on my left breast and holds it for a moment, staring into space. Then he takes his hand away and reaches into a box. He pulls out something pink. "I would say a thirty A would do it, don't you agree, Jean?" Without looking at me, he suddenly becomes very businesslike, hands her the bra, and walks away. My mother shoves it into my hand. She's frowning, but I can see her eyes are wet and shiny.

My face is burning, my throat is dry. I want to disappear. I want to die. For a long moment, I don't know where I am. I don't hear my mom telling me to snap out of it and come into the dressing room. She drags me by the arm into the small cubicle.

"Take off that sweatshirt and stick out your arms," she orders. She's holding the stiff pink bra in front of me. I stare at the wall until it begins to dissolve into bright spots before my eyes and I feel myself floating away from the dressing room and my mother. She slaps me on the back, and I come down to earth with a jolt.

"Stop that staring and stand up straight!" she orders.

She yanks the sweatshirt over my head, then hooks my bare chest into the tight band of cloth. When I take a breath, my ribs strain against the new harness. My breasts are imprisoned by two stiff pink cups, size 30 A.

"Jean!" Mr. Conklin's voice booms down from the mezzanine. "You have a customer." When I look up he sees me, then turns away.

My mother's hands shake when she unhooks the bra. "Take the thing off and put on your sweatshirt. I'll bring it home tonight. I have to go now."

"Maggie," Mr. Conklin calls again, "Mildred is out

back. She wants you to go out and play. Jean, did you hear me? You have a customer."

"Yes, I heard you."

My mother takes me by the shoulders and looks into my eyes. "Bastard!" she says, and places a trembling kiss on my lips. She hurries out of the dressing room. I pick my sailor hat up from the floor and see myself in the mirror as I set it on my head. I look different. My eyes look funny. Not like I'm going to cry, but hollow and old, like my mom's eyes. I look away.

I'll go find Grandma and we'll go home. Grandma will make us a cup of Postum and a piece of cinnamon toast. Maybe she'll want me to give her a manicure—something I only do to be nice, filing her nails, which look like tiny washboards, and covering them with clear polish. Or she might want me to help her do her lessons in the Quarterly, marking passages with blue chalk and sticking the little numbers on the pages of the book that says that God is Mercy, God is Love. Grandma always knows how to say things that make me feel better. Maybe I will even try to tell her what has happened, but I don't think so. I'll never be able to tell anyone. All I know is that I hate Mr. Conklin, and that my hate didn't stop him from doing what he did to me.

Mr. Conklin is coming down from the mezzanine. He stops me before I put my foot on the first stair.

"No, no. Your grandma has gone home. I told her you were going to stay and play out back with Mildred. Go ahead. She's waiting for you." He opens the back door of the store and ushers me out onto a small lawn.

After the dimly lit store, the sunshine on the green grass hurts my eyes. Mildred is standing in the middle of the lawn, the backyard of her large house that faces the street behind. She's doubled over, laughing.

"I seen you!"

"What? Where?"

"In the dressing room! I seen you!"

"You did not!"

"I did too, I seen you from the mezzanine—"

"You're a liar!"

"Oh, yeah? I even know what size you got—thirty A!"

"You do not!"

". . . and it's pink!"

"That's a lie!"

"I don't lie!"

I swing on Mildred, smack her in the mouth with a left hook, follow through with a right to her stomach. She falls to the ground. I stand over her with my dukes cocked. "You take that back!"

"Quit it! I'll tell my daddy! *Daddy!*" she cries, but

the cries are muffled, for she's afraid of me and is hiding her face in the grass. She doesn't move, just lies there sobbing away. Suddenly I'm very, very tired. I want to go home.

"*You—you're a—you're a big fat brick outhouse!*" I say, and begin to run toward the back alley that comes out between the bakery and the Ritz Theater.

I turn to see my new sailor hat flying my way. I grab it and jam it on my head. I wipe my runny nose on the sleeve of my too-small sweatshirt. When I come out of the alley onto the sidewalk, I hear the rumble of roller skates, and Buddy twirls in front of me and skids to a halt.

"What happened to your hat?" His hat is sitting, according to our regulations, two fingers above his left eyebrow.

I look at my new sailor hat, see the smears of green stain. It looks like Mildred has stomped it into the grass.

"I had a fight with Mildred."

His eyes light up. "Yeah? No kiddin'? Who won, you or Flabby Conklin? As if I didn't know."

I shrug. Something tells me this is not a time to brag, not even to Buddy, who has been my friend since fifth grade when, the first time we played, he let me win all his marbles.

"I gotta go, my grandma is waiting," I say.

"Yeah, okay, see ya." He touches his fingers to his hat in our special salute.

I let my fingers slide over my left eyebrow. "Yeah," I say, "see ya."

Uncle Lester is straddling a chair backward at the kitchen table, drinking coffee and reading the sports page of the afternoon *Oregon Journal*. He's wearing his green letterman sweater with the four yellow stripes, his way of telling everybody he was the star fullback at the University of Oregon, what he calls the Big Man on Campus. He's awful conceited, especially since he used to have his picture in the papers all the time running at the camera with the football tucked under his arm, his big hand stretched toward the camera, ready to strong-arm the photographer.

Grandma, who has taken off her navy straw hat and is wearing her gingham housedress now, has a skein of black yarn wrapped around the back of another chair and is rolling it into a tight ball.

"I looked for you to come home with me, but Mr. Conklin told me you were playing with Mildred. Did you have a nice time?"

"It was okay." I never like to bother Grandma with my troubles. Besides, she wouldn't like it that I've been fighting. She likes everything nice and peaceful.

Uncle Lester drops the newspaper onto the floor. His eyebrows shoot up and his mouth drops open. "What? You mean you were playing with that fat slob? I thought you had more class than that!"

He bounces out of the chair and straight-arms me with a quick flat-handed jab to my forehead, knocking my hat to the floor. Laughing, he jabs again. "But I shouldn't be so surprised (jab-jab), you're (jab-jab) two of a kind. You're both built (jab-jab) like a couple brick (jab)—"

"Lester, I told you to stop that kind of talk in this house!"

"Who, me?" He makes a lunge for me.

My fist makes a cracking sound when it catches him in his Adam's apple. He groans and grabs his throat. He croaks, "Think you're pretty tough, don't you? Huh? Huh? Huh?" He's holding me away from him with one hand as he jabs at my head with the other. My fists fan the air in the wide space between us.

"Oh, Lester, stop it! You're making her cry." Grandma sounds like she's crying, which makes me cry harder, for I've never seen Grandma cry, not even when Grandpa died, and I know she loved Grandpa a whole lot. Mama says her English background gives Grandma a stiff upper lip. I can't tell by looking at her. Grandma's lips always seem soft and smiling to me.

Uncle Lester hits me again. Grandma cries, "Lester! I said stop! You are hurting her!"

"No, I'm not, she likes it. Don't you, Maggie? You like it, don't you?" He grabs me in a bear hug, presses his face close to mine, and slides a wet open kiss hard against my lips. I feel his tongue stabbing at my lips and teeth, then pushing deep inside. I stomp my foot down hard on his instep. He releases me with a howl.

"Oh my Gawd! She's about killed me!" He collapses on the floor, rocking and moaning, hugging his foot to his chest.

"Serves you right. Now leave her alone!" Grandma is still crying.

Then, as I run outside, something sails over my head and lands in the zinnias.

Uncle Lester hollers in a singsong voice, "Bye-bye, crybaby! Here's your hat! What's your hurry, lardbutt? Hey, lardbutt, I said what's your hurry?"

My Buddy, Buddy Riley

Buddy Riley lives right next door with his grandma, Mrs. Polanski, and his big brother, Jacob. Who knows what happened to their mom and dad? I don't ask Buddy, and he doesn't ask me how come my brothers and I live only with our mom. There are certain things friends don't ask one another. But everyone else Buddy and me know seems to have both a mama who doesn't work and a daddy who comes home at night. Nobody we know in school has a mom who's divorced—which is nothing to brag about—and nobody else is being raised by a grandma, especially one as peculiar as Mrs. Polanski. It isn't only her long black skirt and the way she talks that make her seem so strange, it's the black laced boot with the thick wooden sole she wears on her club left foot. We know these things make Buddy and me different, and besides, living right next door to each other, we just naturally became friends.

We like to do almost all the same stuff anyhow, like when it isn't raining, we stay after school and play football, and when it is raining we play basketball in the gym. I'm the only girl that plays sports with the boys after school, and even though I'm next to the shortest girl in my class (my friend Tomi Katayama is shorter), I'm as good as any boy at making baskets. Buddy, a year and a half older than me, is the smallest boy in our class, but he's so good at stealing the ball from under the big guys' longer legs, he can dribble the whole length of the gym and sink his famous hook shot before anyone can catch him.

After the game we walk the eight blocks to First Street, where we are now renting the old brown shingled house next door to his grandma's, the one that has his dead grandpa's old Essex parked in front and their milk goat, Freda, in a shack out back.

In the summer in Buddy's backyard, where Freda has chomped the weeds down to dirt, I give Buddy boxing lessons. We wear real boxing gloves that used to belong to Frankie. After my mom's divorce I claimed them for my own. Everyone knows Frankie is not the boxing type, even though Daddy tried since Frankie was three years old to teach him what it takes to become a real man.

But I liked to fight with Daddy. When he was drinking, he bragged that I, Maggie, Margaret Mary Morrison, was the female James J. Braddock, the Pride of the Irish and onetime champion boxer of the world, until Joe Louis knocked him out, and more of a boy than Frankie ever was. When I was little that made me feel special, even though I knew what Daddy said wasn't true. It only takes one good look at me to know I'm a girl, especially now that I have to wear that harness around my chest every day.

I insist on teaching Buddy what my daddy called "The Manly Art of Self-defense, with Marquis of Queensberry Rules," so he can get back at his older brother Jacob, who lifts Buddy by the back of his belt and hangs him on the doorknob where their grandma's flannel nightgown hangs behind the bathroom door. Buddy says the nightgown smells of garlic, which she makes everyone wear on a string around their necks in the winter to ward off evil spirits. But it doesn't seem to be any help when it comes to Jacob. I not only can't teach Buddy to defend himself, but I can't even teach him to land enough jabs to make Jacob lay off him. I'm good with my dukes, and if you don't believe me, ask my little brother, Danny. He knows that if you're boxing with Maggie Morrison, the best self-defense is the manly art of turning your back and running like h-e-double toothpicks. Or better yet, don't be dumb enough to let me talk you into tying on those purple leather gloves in the first place.

My boxing talent is one of the main reasons all the boys, except Johnny Baker, like me. I'm not afraid to fight. I prove it my first day at the new school when I knock out Johnny's front tooth. I don't do it just to show off. I do it as a favor to my cousin Dottie Mae, who asks me to beat him up because he's making fun of her daddy, who has a wooden leg and is the school janitor. My uncle Harry has to drag his leg alongside and swing it forward as he sweeps the school's black pine floors with his wide broom. When my mom finds out what I've done, she guarantees me she'll find a way to knock the meanness out of me or she'll sure as hell die trying. I tell her I only hit Johnny once, and yes, I'm sorry, and yes, I'm ashamed. Then I have to agree that being sorry and ashamed won't bring back Johnny's front tooth, will it? And even though I say no, it won't, so far it hasn't stopped me from using my fists the way my daddy taught me.

One time, when Buddy dropped his guard, my left jab caught him just right. It gave him a bloody nose. He pretended to ignore it, and I did too. I didn't want to see the damage I'd done. There are lots of things I'd rather ignore, like my awful secret, that I also bleed sometimes, and have to wear a thick pad of stiff cotton in my crotch for five days each month, which rubs me raw when I run for a touchdown or hook a shot into the basket.

Buddy is as mad as I am when the principal makes me quit playing with the boys after school. Neither of us knows why I'm being kicked out of the gym, except for what Mr. Pearson says, which is that now I am becoming a young lady. Which I know right away has to be all my mother's fault for making me wear that ugly pink bra, which Mildred Conklin called "Maggie's brass ear!"

Last summer, Buddy and me combed the dusty weeds along the highway for Royal Crown Cola bottles to sell for money to buy our roller skates. We play street hockey on days so hot the metal wheels sink into the soft tar, the same tar we break off and chew like the penny paraffin wax whistles we buy at the candy store and suck dry of the colored sugar water inside.

We prize our sailor hats and special salutes and make our plans to join the navy and see the world, even though everybody knows they are never going to let any girl join the regular navy. We love the military movies full of danger and heroes like Pat O'Brien, James Cagney, and Dennis Morgan, who is my favorite because I like his crooked smile, which is like Buddy's. On Saturdays we sit through the same movie twice.

Buddy also has a year-round Saturday job exercising Mr. Johnson's two old Shetland ponies. Sometimes Buddy rides Old Bob to my house, towing Old Jim behind so I can ride too. After we graduate from B. W. Barnes Junior High next May he is going to ask Mr. Johnson to help him get a job exercising Thoroughbreds at the horse farm in Orenco. Buddy's going to be a professional jockey. He doesn't seem to be growing anymore, so we're sure he'll be perfect for the job. At fourteen and a half Buddy is still the smallest boy in class. In fact, it looks like he's stopped growing altogether. I am a year and a half younger, but I'm still growing, especially in certain places. Even Tomi Katayama is slightly taller than Buddy now.

We're sitting on my back porch watching Buddy's goat, Freda, gnaw on an old stump. It's a cold and misty Sunday afternoon. Then Danny comes running out of the house, shouting that we have been attacked.

"Maggie! You gotta come listen! We've been bombed!"

Buddy says, "You're crazy."

"No, no! Honest! It's true! I just heard it on Frankie's radio!"

"Danny, what were you doing playing with Frankie's radio?" I scold him. "He'd mow you down if he found out."

Frankie has been stationed up north at Fort Lewis, Washington, going on bivouacs with the 42nd Rainbow Division of the National Guard for almost a year, training to go to the Philippines. He'd begged Mama to sign his permission papers so he could go with his two buddies who are older. She'd said he was too young, but he kept begging, and she finally signed. Now Frankie, who didn't like to fight and who Daddy used to call a real sissy, is a soldier in a real war. Daddy was wrong.

Danny says, "He won't find out if you don't tell him, Maggie. You gotta come! The guy said that all our big ships—you know, destroyers and everything—are sunk in a harbor in Hawaii, and he said we're in a real war now! A real war, Maggie!"

Buddy nudges me. "C'mon, let's go listen!"

"Hey! You know my mom doesn't allow any kids in our house."

"But Maggie, it's a war!"

Danny says, "Buddy's okay, Maggie. I won't tell Mama. You gotta come listen right now. Quick!"

I lead the way.

Frankie's room is upstairs and off to one side of the attic. It's decorated with long strings of Frankie's collection of a million different-colored matchbooks, which are stretched across the room just below the ceiling. On the radio a band is playing "The Star-Spangled

Banner." Hearing our national anthem makes me feel like I should be standing at attention and saluting, but since Buddy and me aren't wearing our sailor hats, I just sit very stiff and don't move a muscle.

Side by side we sit on the edge of Frankie's narrow cot, staring at the little square dial of the radio with its cracked wooden case. Last year Frankie traded his almost-brand-new football shoes for the radio. Frankie is no athlete, at least not on the football field, or in the boxing ring. He's more of an inside-the-house-necking-on-the-couch kind of guy. Sometimes after school, when Mama is at work and Frankie thinks he's going to be home alone, some girl will drop by the house. But I usually walk in on them. He hates that.

In a corner stands his prized pair of filthy once-yellow cords, stiff as a board, the legs almost black with dirt and grease and kids' autographs scrawled all over in blue ink. They make me wonder what any girl could ever see in Frankie.

Buddy reaches over to stroke the cords. I can see he wishes he had a pair just like them.

"Don't touch them!" I say.

Buddy quickly puts his hand in his pocket. "Why not? What's wrong with them?"

"They're contagious. They've got cooties."

Danny asks, "Whaddya mean, cooties?"

I refuse to answer. The national anthem hasn't stopped playing yet.

We listen to the announcer's report again about the ships being sunk by Japanese bombs. I don't know what to think. Hawaii is a long way from Oregon, and Japan is even farther than that. I wonder what Tomi and her big brother, Shoji, are thinking. Sometimes on Saturdays Buddy and me, on our way back from returning Old Jim and Old Bob to Mr. Johnson's farm, we stop by Tomi's farm out on the highway past the city park. Sometimes Tomi is working in the field with Shoji and their mom and dad. Last spring she showed us how to plant asparagus in deep trenches of black soil. She told us it will take three years before the plants will be ready to harvest for market.

The next day at school we listen to President Roosevelt tell us on the radio that we are at war with Japan. Tomi is sitting at the desk behind me. I wonder what she's thinking, but we don't say anything to each other.

Along with a bunch of other boys in high school, Buddy's big brother, Jacob, quits school and hitchhikes into Portland to join the navy. But before the navy will take him, he has to talk his grandma into signing the permission slip because, like Frankie, Jacob is only seventeen. However, he doesn't have any trouble getting Mrs. Polanski to sign. She doesn't like the way he never cuts kindling for the breakfast fire and even dares to sass her back. Buddy says she just said, "Goot reed-dance." The day before he leaves for boot camp Jacob moves his grandfather's black '29 Essex out back beyond the clothesline next to Freda's goat shed, for safekeeping.

He tells Buddy, "I ain't gonna need it where I'm goin', and if I get myself killed and don't come back I'm leaving it to you in my will. But until then, you don't dare drive it—you get me, shrimp?" He grabs Buddy by the neck of his sweatshirt, lifts him off the ground, and shoves his face into Buddy's face like he's a real Jimmy Cagney type of tough guy. Then he holds him out at arm's length and watches as Buddy swings a left hook and misses, swings and misses, Buddy's face happy and laughing with the maybe-future inheritance from his big brother, Jake.

That evening Buddy stands in front of my house and gives his shrill two-note whistle. I'm behind my mom watching her stir the spaghetti sauce. I try to whistle back through my thumb and index finger, which I've been practicing practically in my sleep, but I can't do it the way Buddy can. Still, it's a strange loud squeak that makes my mom jump. "Jeez Louise! Not in the house! I about jumped out of my skin. Do that outside."

I'm already out the front door. "Hi, I gotta eat. Whaddya want?"

Buddy slouches up the cement walk and slumps on the bottom step. He finds a pebble and tosses it toward the streetlight on the corner. It lands in the middle of the street. He looks around his feet for a larger piece. Finally he says, "Jake's goin' into the navy tomorrow."

"Yeah, I figured." I come down the steps and sit beside Buddy. I lean forward, searching the ground.

"He says he's goin' to San Diego for boot camp, and then he's goin' overseas."

"Well, sure, that's what they all do. I bet Frankie's already gone. I bet he's on a boat somewhere out on the ocean going to that war already."

"Yeah, but he's been in the National Guard for over a year."

"So what? Now he's in the army. Same thing."

"Yeah, well, Jake's in the navy. He's going to be on a ship."

"Well? That's good! That's where I'd want to be. Wouldn't you?"

Buddy's fingers scrape the cement, gathering small rocks. "Ships get sunk by subs and planes and other ships—you know, torpedoes and bombs and stuff like that."

I say, "Well, sure. We both know that." I find a small rock and toss it into the street.

"Jake can't swim," Buddy says, his voice low.

"You're kidding! Everybody knows how to swim."

"Not Jake."

"Not even dog paddle?"

"Maybe a little bit, but he's afraid of the water. He don't say so, but I just know."

"Well, what's he doing in the navy then, Buddy? How come he didn't join the army like Frankie?"

"He didn't wanna get shot at."

"Buddy! You just said yourself that ships get sunk. People drown or get blown up!"

"Yeah, I know." Buddy's head is so low it's almost touching his shoes. I hardly hear what he says next. "He says if that happens to him, I get to keep the car."

I'm hungry and it's already getting dark. Down on the corner of First and Baseline the streetlight comes on. There's a soft mist in the air—it gives the round globe a yellow halo.

"Okay, I remember that. So what's the big problem? Don't you wanna keep the car?"

Buddy shrugs. I've seen Buddy out my kitchen window while I'm doing the dishes at night. He'll be behind the wheel of Jake's old car, sitting so still you'd hardly know he was there, thinking about the car or

Jake, or both. I know how much Buddy loves that old car of his grandpa's. I'm not so sure how he feels about Jake. But still, Jake is his big brother.

I say, "Maybe the navy'll teach him how to swim."

Buddy takes a deep breath and gathers a couple of small rocks in his hand. Then he sighs and lets them drop. "Yeah," he says. "They'd better."

On the sidewalk across the street a girl is walking toward the corner streetlight. I recognize her as one of the high-school girls I caught squirming on top of Frankie on the couch while my mom was at work. Frankie warned me I'd be sorry if I told on him, but I told anyway. Mama said it's my job to take care of the house until she gets home, and there they were, messing up the living room, doing that kind of stuff, kissing and rolling around with lipstick all over Frankie's face, his long, black, oily, brilliantined hair hanging in his eyes and his filthy cords all bunched up and sticking out in front. It made me sick.

The girl doesn't wave or say hello to me, so I don't wave or say hello to her.

I say, "Get her. She's so stuck up she'd drown in the rain if she didn't have an umbrella." I tip back my head and put my nose in the air.

But Buddy doesn't laugh. He stands, hunches his shoulders, and jams his hands in his pockets. "I gotta go. Grandma's made *schnecken* and stewed apricots and prunes with cream for Jake's last night home. It's his favorite. See ya."

"Yeah, tell Jake so long."

So Jacob's big old black Essex stands in the weeds that winter behind our house and Mrs. Polanski's, bigger and taller than the goat shed. After Jake leaves for the navy, Danny, who has his reasons for hating Jake, takes some of his gang and sneaks around back. They begin to use the Essex for target practice, shooting the BB guns they've gotten for Christmas.

First the windshield and the headlights are cracked. Then someone pees in the gas tank—Danny isn't saying who—and someone else paints the big black steel fenders and high running boards with pink calamine lotion. The purple-and-red streaks on the wooden spokes of the wheels come from the gentian violet and Mercurochrome Ronnie Rhea has supplied. His dad owns the Rexall drugstore at Second and Main. His parents always give him anything he wants, no questions asked. Ronnie is an only child and a spoiled brat.

When Buddy's grandma comes hobbling out the back door to milk the goat, she stops on the back stoop, drops the bucket, and lets out a scary screech. Danny and his friends like to pretend that Mrs. Polanski is a real witch, but when she lets out that holler, they believe it for sure. One look at her, shorter than Buddy and with her long gray hair fallen out of its bun and blowing in the wind, and her swinging that clubfoot with the four-inch wooden sole forward as she comes at them—well, it's enough to send the boys running and screaming out of her yard. But by then, the damage has been done to Jacob's old car.

When Buddy discovers the mess, he's ready to commit murder. "You tell Danny he'd better stay out of my way, or I'm gonna knock his block off!" It's Saturday morning, and he's riding Old Bob. Behind him Old Jim, head lowered, snuffles the weeds in our front yard.

I force my fingers through Old Jim's shaggy blond mane. "Okay, I'll tell him, and I'll tell my mom. She'll take his gun back to the store, for sure."

"Why'd he do that? I never done nothin' to Danny."

I say, "Yeah, Buddy, I know. But it's not you, it's Jake. You know how he used to chase Danny and just about burn a hole in his skull, giving him a Dutch rub all the time? Especially right after Danny got a haircut?"

Buddy rubs the top of his head. "Yeah, he used to do that to me too."

"Well, then?"

"Yeah, well, it may be Jake's car officially, but doggonit, I'm in charge of it now! It's my car until the war is over!"

So the broken-down old Essex sits all winter among the backyard weeds in the rain. Early in the spring, when we are having a few good days of sunshine, we go out to look it over. Most of the calamine lotion has washed off the fenders, and the inside upholstery has begun to dry. But there isn't much Buddy can do about the cracked windshield and headlights.

"You tried to start it up yet?" I ask.

"Naw."

"Why not?"

"Grandma won't let me."

"How do you know if it'll still run?"

"I don't. They coulda ruined the whole engine. If Jake comes home now, he'll kill me for sure."

"Isn't he coming home for a furlough or something?"

"Naw."

"Why not?"

"He's in the brig at the Brooklyn Navy Yard."

"Why? What'd he do?"

"Hit somebody—an officer."

"Oh, boy, he sure shouldna done that." Buddy and me, we know you don't do anything with an officer but salute and follow orders. But Jacob? Like I said, he's big enough and mean enough, but even he can't be that stupid, can he? "How come?" I ask.

Buddy sits on the running board, shaking his head. "I dunno. He says he'll write us another letter later. All I know is, I gotta get this car fixed, or he's going to kill me good and dead."

There's no way to know what Danny and his gang have done to the engine. When Buddy puts his nose to the hole, sniffing for any gas in the tank, his head jerks back. "Pee-you!"

"What?"

"It still stinks like piss."

I say, "Yep, that's gotta be Danny, all right." He and Frankie left enough on the floor around the toilet for me to know what he's talking about. I don't have to put my nose in a hole.

Jacob writes Buddy from the brig at the Brooklyn Navy Yard to go ahead and start up the car once in a while so the battery won't go dead. One day, when I'm waiting for him outside his kitchen door, Buddy makes a fast grab for the key from the nail beside the kitchen mirror and heads out the back door.

"Here! Vere you tink you go mit dat?" His grandma is holding the battered bucket, ready to go out to milk the goat.

"I gotta start up Jacob's car."

"You touch dat contraption, you're gonna git vot for."

"I'm only going to start it so's the battery don't die, Grandma," he says.

"So, God forbid, it should die, but how?"

"It's the battery, Grandma, that starts the engine— you know, like the light switch turns on the electric light?"

She squints at him, giving him that look Buddy calls her Evil Eye. He freezes at attention for a long moment. Then his grandma gives a quick short nod and points a finger at him. "You do anyting else, Rudolph Isaac Riley, und you know vot you git."

"Yes, ma'am."

Buddy bolts past me, clutching the key. I follow after him. We plow through the wet grass, and Buddy climbs up into the front seat. He sticks in the key and gives it a turn. After a lot of grinding and sputtering, the car backfires three times and dies.

Buddy smiles. "Hot damn! The battery's not dead. I was worried about that."

Mrs. Polanski watches from the back porch. She waves the milk bucket at him. "Vot's de madder vit dat ting?"

Buddy stretches himself tall in the driver's seat. "It won't start, Grandma. It's deader'n a doornail."

"How so it is so? Vot you mean?"

"It's dead. One of them kids peed in the gas tank."

"Oy gevalt! Dem little hellions—dey killed Jacob's car mit da pee?"

"I think it's just out of gas, Grandma."

"Vell den, leaf it alone, da poor dead ting. Go git me Freda and bring her to here."

"But, Grandma, the car's got to have gas before we'll know if it's been wrecked or not."

She raises her voice to a small screech. "You go git me dat gotdam nanny goat, you Rudolph Isaac boy."

Buddy runs to the back of the lot, pulls up Freda's stake from under the clothesline, and jerks the goat toward the old woman. When he stakes Freda again in the weeds beside the steps, he begs, "Grandma, please, please?"

She glares down at him, her chin raised. "Und zo vere iss mine stool?"

Buddy takes the steps two at a time, rushes into the kitchen, runs out again with the three-legged stool, places it on the ground behind Freda. He waits for his grandma to gather her long skirt and sit.

"Grandma, now—please, please!"

"So, go, go, vot's to be keepin you?"

"But I need some money for gas."

His grandma has pressed her forehead into the stiff furry butt of Freda and is hanging on to the goat's two tits like they are handlebars, pulling and squirting milk into the battered bucket between her knees. Her club-foot is stretched straight beside the goat's left flank. When Freda lifts a hind leg to kick Mrs. Polanski, Mrs. Polanski swings her clubfoot like a baseball bat. It sounds like a home run when her toe slams into Freda's ribs. "You tink I don't know who's da boss around here, maybe?" she says, and kicks the goat again.

Buddy throws his arms in the air and runs around the house. He enters the front door and steals a quarter out of his grandma's pocketbook.

"I'm going with you," I say, running after him.

"No! Stay here and guard my car!" he hollers, and takes off running two blocks to the Texaco station on Baseline Highway.

I stay behind, watching Mrs. Polanski, whose eyes are closed and whose head is still resting on Freda's butt, when Buddy comes panting into the backyard dragging the heavy gas can. He pours the two gallons into the tank. Together we lean in, our noses close to the gas tank, and sniff like two hungry dogs at the delicious fumes of ethyl gasoline.

Finally Buddy climbs into the driver's seat. This time, when he sets the spark and twists the ignition key, I jump in on the other side. The Essex coughs and sputters and quits and coughs again, and suddenly jerks to a start.

"Hot diggety dog!" Buddy crows, and stretches his leg to jam his foot on the clutch, crams it into gear, gives it gas again, and the big car shoots forward.

"Whoa!" he hollers when the bumper hits the wood-pile. It isn't just a nudge, but a hard bump that pushes and tumbles the stack of cordwood near our back porch. Buddy finds the brake, then the clutch. He grinds the gears up and down until he lands on the one that lets the car back up.

Old Mrs. Polanski, her head pressed into Freda's butt, is milking in her sleep, but Freda is wide awake. She kicks at the bucket and misses. She gets slammed in the ribs again for her trouble. Mrs. Polanski doesn't miss a stroke, just keeps on napping and dragging on Freda's shriveled tits.

Buddy turns the wheel again, aiming the Essex toward the space between our two houses and the street. When he accidentally presses his foot too hard on the gas pedal, the car suddenly shoots backward and hits one of the wooden poles of his grandma's clothesline. We hear the crack of splitting wood at the same moment Buddy's wet overalls, Mrs. Polanski's heavy black dress, and somebody's long winter underwear flop to the ground.

Quickly, in turn, Buddy pumps the brake, the clutch and the gas pedal, and somehow finds the right gear. At last Jacob's car lurches out of the backyard past our kitchen window, between the two houses, and bounces off the curb onto First Street.

The old Essex rattles and the engine clinks and clanks and roars. We are going way too fast. I hang on to the seat and hold my breath, and forget to say a single word. Buddy is red in the face and pulling back on the big steering wheel the way he does on Old Bob's reins once in a while, but it looks like that isn't what you do to slow down that old Essex. I can tell Buddy needs time to get his heels into that old car and make it do what he wants. But it's getting away from him. Finally I can't keep quiet another minute. So, like Buddy, I holler, "Whoa!"

Then, as the sun brightens and the clouds grow fluffier, Buddy straightens his back, squares up the steering wheel, and carefully aims the car down the middle of the quiet street. He's found the brake. The car slows down just enough for us to relax, sit back, and enjoy our ride. Like a good jockey, it seems he's gotten his grandpa's old car to settle down and know who's in charge. I can tell he has the hang of it real good now like they've become one mind and one machine, you might say. So me and Buddy, him with a big wide grin on his face, proceed down First Street, away from the town and Danny and Mrs. Polanski and Freda and the war.

Not in any hurry whatsoever to head back home.

Mr. Johnson's Pasture

After a week of rain, the sun is so hot that thin wisps of steam rise from the wet ground beneath Maggie's bare feet. She looks up at the bright blue sky. Not a single cloud today, black or white. Yesterday was the Fourth of July so naturally it had to rain. How come it always rains on the Fourth of July? It can be 110 in the shade on the *third* of July, but just let it be the *Fourth* of July and it rains cats and dogs! The Tilt-a-Whirl and the Octopus are no fun when your socks get soggy and the soft steady rain soaks your sweatshirt like a sopping wet dishrag. Naturally, now that the carnival is at this moment packing up all the rides and leaving town, here comes the sun.

Maggie nudges a clod of black mud off the bottom of her foot with her other big toe. Her feet are cold and muddy. Nothing is going to warm up this ground today. She should've worn shoes, but the sidewalks were warm and dry when they left town, and Buddy doesn't seem to mind—the soles of his feet are hard as boards. But then, Buddy is always barefoot in the summer, especially when he exercises Mr. Johnson's Shetland ponies. His heels shine like old leather when he rides Old Bob in his jockey crouch, his butt high in the air.

Buddy, astride Old Bob, stretches his lips tight against his front teeth and aims his whistle at Old Jim standing beneath the weeping willow tree.

Maggie stretches her own lips, curls her tongue, and shoves it hard into the back of her front teeth. She blows until her dimples ache.

Buddy grins his crooked-toothed grin. "You sound like a tire goin' flat. You're never gonna get it."

"Leave me alone, I know how. I'm just a little out of practice."

She keeps her eyes on Old Jim and tightens her cheeks to blow again. Old Jim is grazing now. Wisps of steam almost hide his hooves in the short grass. He doesn't raise his head or flick his ears. It's been almost a year since Maggie has been out to Mr. Johnson's farm to see Old Jim and Old Bob. She tries again to blow.

"You look just like my grandma with her teeth out."

Light-headed, Maggie gives up.

Buddy gives another whistle, and here comes Old

Jim, ambling and stumbling toward Old Bob and Buddy. Buddy jumps down off the pony and slips a halter over Jim's gray muzzle. He stands beside Jim's sagging belly, his hands cupped.

"I know how to get on. I don't need any help," she says.

She pushes past him and grabs the pony's mane. With a grunt and a quick hop, she lands solid on Old Jim's back.

Buddy groans.

"What now?" she asks.

Buddy lifts himself into the curve of Bob's spine. He lands as light as a feather. He rubs his hand over Old Bob's neck, busy smoothing the damp coat.

"Well, what?" Maggie insists.

Buddy nudges Old Bob with a bare heel, and the pony begins to walk. Maggie prods Old Jim to follow.

"What's wrong with you, anyhow?" Her heel gives an extra sharp kick into Old Jim's ribs.

"Nothin'. You just landed a little hard, that's all."

When she catches up, she says, "I never said I was as good as you. You're the one who's going to be the jockey."

Buddy hunches his narrow shoulders and drops them, shrugging off an answer.

"Besides, you're older and been doing this a lot

longer—it's your job." She's glad it isn't hers. She isn't going to admit that Jim's spine feels like a row of sharp rocks under her rump, or that his legs seem to be shorter, somehow.

Her heels find a soft spot in his belly. "Move!" she commands again. She jabs and rocks forward until Jim begins to snort and blow before he finally takes a step. He tries to trot to keep up with Old Bob. As she bounces, Maggie's tailbone feels like it's caught in a nutcracker.

She hollers, "Whoa! Whoa! Buddy, wait!"

Buddy reins in and turns. "What?"

"Hold on, don't go so fast!"

"I'm not. You're just out of practice, that's all."

"I am not. But wait a minute. Can't we walk them first?"

"I got to trot them, Maggie. That's my job. Why don't you just wait with Jim while I trot Bob a little ways, then we'll trade and you can walk Bob to the corral."

She moves herself back onto Jim's haunches. "I didn't walk all this way in my bare feet just to watch you ride, Buddy Riley!"

Buddy is quiet. Maggie ignores him. She needs time to think.

Buddy isn't acting like his natural self. He isn't

giving her his usual straight look. She saw that same look on his face when Miss Cornelius sent him to the principal's office for practicing his whistle in class, after the whistle worked for the first time. The principal, Mr. Pearson, opened his top desk drawer and showed Buddy the famous piece of red rubber hose he keeps there for times just like that.

Maggie blows softly through the narrow trough she's made with her tongue. A low moan like the north wind whistling around a corner makes her forget her anger at Buddy. She smiles at him.

He's chewing on his lower lip, then sucking away.

"So, how about it, Maggie?"

"Buddy, you're acting like you don't want me to ride Old Jim. How come?"

"Forget it. It's nothin'."

"I been coming here with you for three years now—"

"I know, I just thought if it bothers you—well, never mind, forget it."

He gives Old Bob another soft poke with his heels that sends him into a trot; then he hooks his knees tight just below Bob's neck, lowers his head to one side, and crouches forward. With his rump high in the air like that, he looks just like a real jockey. His rump is still in the air when he trots back to her.

She asks, "When are you going to the Thoroughbred farm and ask for that job?"

"I don't know."

"Why not go today?"

"I keep thinking, what if I start to grow all of a sudden? You know, suddenly get too tall?"

"Why would you do that now?"

Buddy shrugs and licks his lip. "Who knows? My brother's five foot six."

"So what? Jacob's always been bigger than you."

"Maybe I'm just a slow starter."

"Now you're talking dumb. Look at Frankie. He's six foot three and weighs a hundred and forty pounds. And look at me. Do I look like I'm ever going to be six foot three and weigh a hundred and forty pounds? Not in a million years. And neither will you."

Buddy smiles at Maggie. "You know it's not the same. You're a girl." He sighs. "Jacob would've given anything to be six foot three—or even six feet. He used to hang himself from his ankles in the goat shed and hold a big sack of sand."

"You're kidding!"

Buddy laughs. "I know it sounds dumb, but he made me tie him up there, then hand him the sack of sand."

"That explains why he's ended up looking like a gorilla. That never works."

"I know, but he thought it would."

"What a moron! He must've been behind the door when the brains were passed out. I can't believe the navy took him—they must really be hard up," Maggie said. "You're a lot smarter and a lot shorter. You'll be a great jockey. How much do you weigh now?"

"Last week I weighed ninety-nine on Mr. Johnson's feed scale."

"Well, then?"

Buddy nods. "Yeah."

"If Mr. Johnson put in a good word for you at the Thoroughbred farm, I bet you'd get that job right away. Let's go ask him." The sooner she gets off Old Jim's bony back the better.

"They're not home. They went into town. Mrs. Johnson's getting some more jars to make strawberry jam."

"Mom says her strawberry jam is as thin as dishwater and just as tasty."

Old Jim is standing quietly with his head drooping to the ground. Buddy says, "He looks like that picture of the tired old Indian's horse that's hanging in the library."

"Except that I'm no Indian," Maggie says, "and Old Jim's got nothing to be tired about. We've hardly gone six feet. Let's go to the barn and wait for Mr. Johnson, okay?" She gives the reins a quick jerk.

"Don't!"

"Don't what?"

"Don't pull so hard."

"I wasn't pulling hard."

"It looked like you were."

"Well, I wasn't. You know I wouldn't do anything to hurt Old Jim." Maggie leans forward and throws her arms around his neck. "Would I, Jim-Jim?"

"It's just that they're getting old. He don't see so good anymore."

Buddy begins to walk Old Bob slowly toward the barn. He whistles at Old Jim. Maggie waits for him to follow. Jim gives a long wheeze but remains standing, his legs locked. Buddy swings back and takes his reins, giving them a gentle tug. Jim begins to move forward very slowly. Then he tosses his head, and the reins slip from Buddy's hand. In a sudden spurt, Old Jim trots past Buddy, his nose aimed toward the barn. To Maggie, it seems like he is flying. She falls backward, then forward, clutching his mane. "Whoa!" she shouts. "Slow down, Jim!" And finally, "Buddy! Help!"

But nothing stops the old pony, even when Maggie feels one of his back legs begin to drag.

"Get off, Maggie!" Buddy hollers. "Get off! It's Mr. Johnson coming home! Jim hears his car . . ."

In a blur she sees the old gray Chevrolet ease into the driveway. She gasps as the gate of the corral comes toward her too fast, too fast! She dives for the ground just as Old Jim crashes and collapses in front of the gate. For a moment his legs thrash at the air and his hard hooves graze her shoulder. Stunned and stiff, Maggie sits up. Old Jim lies like a stone a few feet away. Buddy leaps from the back of Old Bob and kneels beside the dead pony.

"Oh, God, Jim! I'm sorry! He told me! He told me!"

Maggie crawls over to Buddy. "Is he—dead?"

Buddy doesn't answer. Instead, she hears the heavy crunch of footsteps on gravel and looks up into the large red face and fierce blue eyes of Mr. Johnson.

"What the hell do you think you're doing, girl? Get away from him, the both of you!" He brushes past her, grabs Buddy by an arm, and swings him around like a whip. "You little bastard, look what you've done! You've killed the poor old sonofabitch!"

Maggie freezes. She doesn't dare look sideways at Buddy, but she feels him flinch as if he's been hit. Mr. Johnson pokes a toe into Jim's belly. He shakes his head. "Dead as dead!"

"Oh, no." Maggie's words come with a deep sob.

She tries again to speak but is taken with such a chill her teeth begin to chatter. Finally she realizes that Mr. Johnson is shouting at her.

"I said come here, young lady! Come here and take a good look at what you've done to this poor soul."

She moves to stand beside Buddy.

Buddy croaks, "No . . ."

Mr. Johnson towers over the two of them. His clean blue shirt, buttoned at the throat, blouses above the wide brass buckle of his belt. His trousers, once pants to a Sunday suit, shine from many pressings. Maggie, afraid to lift her eyes, notices the tiny gray pinstripes, the narrow cuffs that end just above thick ankles, the frayed red threads of a small design on the thin dress stockings. His wide black shoes turn up at the toes like small bobsleds. Buddy, standing before him, looks so small that for a brief moment Maggie can only think of her little brother, Danny.

"Don't try to deny it—and I'm not through with you either, young man, not by a long shot!" He unbuttons his shirt cuffs and rolls his sleeves to the elbows. Then he crosses his arms. "I left it up to you to tell her. I trusted you to take care of it, didn't I?"

"Yess-s-s-sir."

"And what did you do? Did you tell her?"

"No—nossir."

Mr. Johnson's blue eyes flick onto Maggie's, then drill into Buddy's again. His chest heaves beneath his heavy arms. When he speaks, his words come slowly.

"Old Jim is dead because of you."

Hot tears spring from Maggie's eyes. "No!"

Mr. Johnson ignores her, glares at Buddy. "Isn't that right?"

"Y-Y-Yessir."

"How many years you been coming out here, taking care of Old Jim and Old Bob?"

"Four."

"This would be your fifth year working for me?"

"Yessir."

"I always thought you loved them old ponies."

"He did, Mr. Johnson—he does," Maggie sobs. "We both do."

He motions with his head toward the ground. "And now you got a dead pony to prove it. Is this the way you how your love?"

"N-N-Nossir." Buddy chokes.

"A man can't take care of his animals ain't much of a man in my book."

"Please, Mr. Johnson, Buddy didn't . . ."

But Maggie is silenced with a hard glance. Mr. Johnson looks over at Old Bob standing a few feet from Old

Jim's carcass and shakes his head. "Old Bob is going to miss his partner—they been together for a lot of years. How old are you, Maggie?"

Startled, she answers, "Thirteen, almost fourteen."

"And what are you now?" he asks Buddy.

"Fifteen—and a half."

"Those old ponies was older than either one of you—we got them when our girls were six and eight. Now they're both married. Couldn't neither one of them take the ponies, so we kept them here—besides, this is their home."

Mr. Johnson is talking like both ponies are dead. Maggie fights to keep her sobs buried in her chest.

Mr. Johnson heaves a big sigh. "Well, better get Old Bob in the corral and give him some feed. No sense making him stand here like this. When you've finished, I want the both of you to come into the barn. I'm not through with you yet."

They watch Mr. Johnson go in the house.

Maggie says, "Buddy . . ." She wants to tell him she's afraid of Mr. Johnson, she wants to go home. But she can't speak.

Buddy steps around the dead pony to take the reins of Old Bob. She opens the gate and follows them into the corral. She's still silent while Buddy feeds Old Bob.

Mr. Johnson is waiting in the barn. He has changed from his town clothes and is wearing his faded denim overalls, a work shirt, and a pair of old brown boots.

"Come on over here." He kicks a boot at a small brood of yellow banty chicks clustered about his feet. They scatter, then gather again and scurry with the mother hen into an empty cow stall. Mr. Johnson is a berry farmer and has a packing shed on the other side of the house and nine acres of strawberries, raspberries, and boysenberries growing in long rows on the sloping land. For the past two summers Maggie and Buddy, with Danny in tow, have caught the school bus in front of the Christian Church on Third Street at six-thirty in the morning to pick Mr. Johnson's berries before the sun is high. He keeps two cows in the barn for the milk and butter, and uses the rest as work space.

"I said, come over here." He's removing a stiff tarp from a rusty iron hay scale. He points a finger at the metal platform. "Get up on that," he tells Buddy.

Buddy steps on the scale. Mr. Johnson watches the weights already in place waver, then settle into balance. He counts the discs to make sure they haven't been changed since the last time; then he nods. "Okay, still the same. Just under the wire. Step down."

He motions to Maggie. "Get up there, young lady. Let's see what's what."

"What for?"

"I need to know something."

"Know what?"

"How much you weigh nowadays." He puts his large hand on her shoulder and leads her to the scale.

Maggie feels her face burn, but she keeps both feet firmly on the barn floor. "I know how much I weigh," she says.

"You do? How much?"

"Probably about the same as Buddy." That was true a year ago. But in the past year she's grown taller than Buddy. Her face gets even hotter with the lie she's just told Mr. Johnson.

"Well, good. If you weigh the same as Buddy, we won't have to change these weights, will we? Step up here and let's find out."

She steps on the scale and closes her eyes. She hears Mr. Johnson rattle some metal around in a box. She takes a peek. The arm of the scale has tipped up and he's attaching another narrow iron weight to it, then another. She closes her eyes again.

"Just what I was afraid of," he mutters to himself. Then, in a quiet voice, "Okay, Maggie. You can step down."

Maggie gives Buddy a sideways look, but his eyes are on the row of weights.

Mr. Johnson says to him, "Now you see?"

Maggie barely hears Buddy answer, "Yessir."

"Didn't I warn you?"

"Yessir."

"You knew them old ponies couldn't carry more than a hundred pounds?"

Buddy nods.

Mr. Johnson slides his hand into the side opening of his overalls and digs into the pocket of his old suit pants. He withdraws a small leather pouch, fishes for two silver quarters. He holds them out to Buddy, who shakes his head and puts his hands behind his back.

"Take it. This covers last month."

Mr. Johnson takes one of Buddy's clenched hands and pries open the fingers. He places the two quarters in the palm. "Take it, and we'll call it even."

Buddy mumbles something and lets the money drop to the floor.

Mr. Johnson slowly bends and retrieves the two coins. "What did you say?"

"I said I didn't earn it."

"Take it anyway."

"No."

"And what is the reason you didn't earn it?"

"I didn't do what you told me."

"Meaning?"

"I shouldn't have let her ride."

Mr. Johnson explodes. "You goddam right you shouldna!" He grabs Buddy's hand again and forces the money into it. "You're going to take this goddam money so's you won't ever forget what you done!"

Just then Maggie hears the high voice of Mrs. Johnson calling into the barn.

"Axel! Come out here, over by the fence! It's Old Jim!"

He hollers back, "Never mind, Melba—"

"What do you mean, never mind! We've got a dead pony out here!" She enters the barn wearing a thin housedress and her bedroom slippers.

"I already know it, Melba. Go back in the house. I'm taking care of it."

She points at Maggie. "It was her, wasn't it? I told you she was developing too fast. I could tell it was happening just by looking at her." She's standing so near, Maggie can smell the sweet sugary scent of overripe strawberries. "She's the one. She killed Old Jim, didn't she?"

"Shut up, Melba, goddammit, and go back into the house!" Mr. Johnson turns again to Maggie and Buddy. "Okay, I've said my piece. You two can leave."

"Axel! At least make them help bury Old Jim. Axel?"

But Maggie has already run out of the barn. Buddy follows more slowly. After he's passed Mrs. Johnson, he runs across the pasture toward the cedar rail fence. When he reaches the path that leads to the back road, Maggie, still running, calls to him, "Buddy! Stop, please stop! Wait for me, Buddy."

He waits by the fence.

When she catches up, she fights to catch her breath. "He wasn't being fair—"

"Yes, he was." He doesn't look at her.

"No! It wasn't your fault. It was mine!"

Buddy shakes his head and looks at the coins in the palm of his hand. "No, Maggie, he was right, it was my fault! All my fault!"

Then, with all his might, Buddy throws the two silver quarters toward that spot under the weeping willow tree where Old Jim used to wait for him, and he runs up the muddy path to the back road.

Next Door to the Poorhouse

Dear Tomi,

I haven't written since I got your last letter because I lost your new address. I'm so mad at myself, Tomi! I know I should have written right back, but with school starting and everything else, all of a sudden my mom gets this bright idea that we're moving *again* and she makes me help pack up all our stuff, so now, in all this mess to unpack, I can't find your letter anywhere. I'm sorry, sorry, sorry! So even though I can't mail any letters to you right now, I'll just keep writing until I hear from you. Then, when I have your new address, I'll send you a whole bunch, okay?

Tomi, I miss you a lot! It's not the same at school now that you're gone. I don't have a real best friend to talk to (boo hoo!). Besides Buddy, that is, but since we don't live next door to each other anymore, I don't see him except at school. Besides, now that we're in high school, Buddy's acting so different. When he gets with Donny and Fritz, they look at us girls funny. Then they get all red in the face and laugh real hard. They act like they're telling dirty jokes, which I think is very disgusting!

Oh, poor little Maggie, as my mama always says. But I know she doesn't mean it because then she says, Why don't you go off in the woods and eat fuzzy worms? She can get real sarcastic sometimes. So I'll just pretend you are still here and I'm just talking to you with my pen, okay?

How do you like it where you are now? I bet it's a lot better than that old cow stall you were living in at the Exposition Grounds when Buddy and I went to see you that time. Boy! It made me so mad! It's not fair, Tomi. How did you all fit in that small space and cook and sleep? And what did Shoji think, having to give up being student body president of our school like that? (I think he's so cute and handsome but *promise* me you won't tell him I said so.) My mom flipped her lid when she found out we hitched a ride into Portland with Mr. Johnson when he went to

see your daddy that Saturday. She wouldn't have
found out if Danny hadn't opened his big trap.
Sometimes he's such a pain. But what can I say? He's
the only brother I've got at home now that Frankie is
gone. Frankie has been in the war for almost a year
already. He's on some island in the Pacific Ocean. He
hasn't sent us a V-mail for quite a while. Today's his
nineteenth birthday.

So, Tomi, are you okay? Well, I'm not! And here's
why! *We've just moved again.* Did I tell you that yet?
I'm getting plenty sick and tired of it. Can you believe we have moved five times in the last five years,
all in the same town, and that's not counting the
three times in between when we moved back in with
Grandma. Sure, we had to move a lot before Mom
got her divorce, but that was because of my dad's
job. We lived in thirteen different places before we
moved here. No kidding, Tomi, I'm beginning to
think my mom is getting a little crazier all the time.
She's never let us have friends over because she
works and says she can't be there to keep an eye on
us. Frankie did it anyhow. I mean, have a girlfriend
over after school so they could neck on the couch
and everything. But that's Frankie.

Anyhow, Tomi, what I'm trying to tell you is that

now we are living on the Baseline Highway itself, not
too far past your truck farm. That is, what used to
be your farm before you had to leave it. I bet you
miss your vegetable gardens this year, and your vegetable stand, or do you have your own gardens where
you are now? I wonder if those people who bought
your farm know about the asparagus you and your
mom planted last year. Do you think they're going to
wait two years for it to be ready to eat?

So guess what? My mom has herself this boyfriend
whose name is Wendall. He's a guy she used to know
in high school. I think she's trying to keep it a secret
from Grandma and Uncle Lester, which explains why
we've moved way out here in the sticks. What makes
me so mad is that just when it begins to feel like we
belong somewhere, like living next door to Buddy,
we move again! When my mom makes up her mind,
though, that's that.

This time Danny and I share a little attic. He gets
one end, I get the other. There's a chimney in the
middle that divides us, and the roof slants down on
both sides. Danny is still the same sneaky little
snooper he's always been, so I don't have any privacy
at all! As usual, he gets into my stuff when I'm not
there, but the other night I caught him peeking at me

when I thought he was asleep and I was getting
ready for bed! Mom wouldn't believe me when I told
her. She thinks I'm always picking on Danny. He's
the baby of the family.

When I tell you where we live now, you're not
going to believe me, Tomi! I bet you'll know exactly
where we are. It's that little house right next door to
the County Poor Farm where all the old people go
who have no place else, and no money. My mom
says if things get any worse around here, she'll just
move next door. I personally don't think she's funny
when she says this, but I laugh anyhow.

My mom needs a lot of encouragement these days.
She hates her job at the store. Some nights when she
gets off the bus, she just sits down at the kitchen
table and cries. Sometimes I get mad at her (but I
never sass her), but other times I just sit down and
cry with her. I can't help it. And if Danny isn't up at
Lonny's helping to milk the cows, he sits down and
cries too. We hug her and pat her and say everything's going to be okay. I pour her a cup of coffee,
if I've made it, and she lights a Chesterfield and sips
her coffee. Then she tells me to get her some toilet
paper so she can blow her nose, and we all begin to
dry our eyes and blow our noses. She gives a big

sigh and tells Danny to check the fire in the stove,
see if it needs a stick of wood, and we'd better get
something to eat, it's late.

Danny always wants to know what's for dinner.
We eat fried eggs and potatoes, or chipped beef and
milk gravy on toast, which is Mom's favorite, or spaghetti, which is my favorite, or something else. It all
tastes good to me. Except Danny's favorite, hominy,
which tastes like chalk and looks like the dead white
toe I found once on the railroad tracks at Camp One.
I have toast instead, which I brown on the top of the
stove, or I make a one-eyed sandwich in the frying
pan, which we saw Wallace Beery make for Shirley
Temple, remember that movie? Or I have Wheaties.
I'm not choosy. We always have sugar, and fresh
milk from Lonny's cow, which is not like that blue
kind my cousins drink. And real butter. My mom
refuses to use white oleo because she says we might
as well be eating lard.

The landlord left an old Shetland pony in the corral behind the house that Danny is supposed to take
care of. He's lame and dirty and mean, not at all like
the ponies Buddy used to exercise. Danny rides it and
tries to make it gallop around the field but it's old
and all worn out. He says he has more fun riding
Lonny's cows—he twists their tails and makes them

buck. When he comes in sometimes he's wearing cow manure and turkey poop on his shoes and doesn't even notice how he's tracking it in on the linoleum.

Well, I got to go, Tomi. My mom's calling me for supper. I'll write more later, after I've done my Latin (I'm getting all A's. I bet you miss Miss Weathered. She's my favorite teacher in the whole school), and after I do the dishes. Don't you hate to put your hands in cold soapy dishwater when the Ivory Flakes get all scummy and gray on top?

December 7, 1942

Dear Tomi,

I still haven't heard from you and I can't mail this until I know your new address. I can't believe it's almost two months since I wrote last. What's happening? Are you mad at me? Please don't be mad. I am so sorry I lost your address. I've looked and looked but I can't find it in any of my stuff. Please write to me. Please, please? I get kinda lonesome living out here with the only neighbors being the turkey gobblers and the cows up back of us.

Besides, things are not so good right now at our

house. My mom is getting crazier all the time and doing a lot of crying at night when she thinks we are asleep. Danny and me, we just stay real quiet up-stairs. Sometimes Wendall's down there, trying to cheer her up. Danny told me that one night he went down the ladder to go to the bathroom and Wendall was in bed with her but I don't believe him and tell him he must've been sleepwalking again. He does that sometimes and ends up peeing in the broom closet. But he swears on a stack of Bibles it's the truth. (We don't have real Bibles, we just say that.) I'm not sure, though. Danny may be a real sneak, but he's no liar. And Wendall is here a lot now that we live out in the sticks.

Sometimes when he comes he brings his daughter, Beverly, and she stays with Danny and me while they go for a drive in his Terraplane sedan. They always say they are going to bring us back a quart of ice cream, but lots of times they forget, or the ice cream is all runny. I know you won't tell anyone so I can tell you the truth, Tomi. I'm not sure I like Wendall, and I know *for sure* I don't like his daughter, Beverly, not one bit! Mom says for me to please be nice to her, and not to rock the boat.

Not that I would want to rock any boat with Bev-erly in it. I'd be the one to drown! She's a year older

than me and almost six feet tall, and she must weigh
a ton! Nobody can push her around, but with me it's
a different story. Have you ever had anyone stand
too close to you and breathe right in your face? She
gets so close her boobs almost touch me and she has
to crick her neck to look down at me. She paints her
face with Max Factor pancake makeup so thick it
looks like it's about to chip off and it still doesn't fill
in those big chuckholes on her nose and cheeks that
are deep enough to hide a hog. She calls me names
like Squirt Nose and Puke Brain and Shithead, and
when I push her away, she laughs and asks me if I
want a knuckle sandwich. Then she slugs me a good
one in my upper arm that paralyzes it for at least an
hour. After, she wants to be real friendly and offers
me a Lucky Strike, which I of course refuse. I promised my grandma, who's very religious, I would never
smoke. Grandma's always so sweet to me, knits me
sweaters and lets me drink Postum and cambric tea
with her sometimes, and tries to teach me how to
play whist. She never gets mad at me when I don't
go to church with her anymore since we moved the
last two times. This is the only thing she has ever
asked me to promise, so I promised. It was easy. I
don't want to smoke now for a million dollars. When
I used to smoke, that was just a kid thing I did five

years ago. I'm growing up now. And besides, I'm a
Girl Reserve, and we have our principles. Do they
have Girl Reserves where you are, Tomi?

Old Beverly, she's been smoking for a whole year
now. Her dad knows and doesn't even care. So when
he takes my mom out for ice cream or to the movies,
she lights up right there in the kitchen. I wave my
hand to make the smoke go away and she just laughs.
I worry that when Mom comes home she will see the
smoke and think I've been smoking too.

I think Wendall is so easy on Beverly because he
doesn't have to take care of her. She lives in Portland
with her mother. Mom says the only time Beverly
comes to see her dad is on the day her child support
money is due. I don't think Mom likes Beverly, but
she's never come right out and said so, and neither
have I. When I tell her about how I get slugged in
the arm all the time, she just says to learn to get
along. One time when she was cranky, she said not
to be such a damn coward and to just hit her right
back. But, Tomi, can you see me hitting Beverly
back? It would be like me trying to knock out a
steamroller with a toothpick. Or me being Popeye
without my spinach! She'd just flatten me like a
pancake.

Danny thinks it's funny. When she offers me a
cigarette and I say no, he always says he'll take it!
But Beverly won't give him one. Of course, he likes
it that Beverly knocks me around because that's what
I do to him sometimes.

Lots of times though, Danny and me, when there's
nothing else to do, we have fun playing our special
games before Mom gets home from work. Like I said,
the house is small, just a living room, kitchen, Mom's
bedroom, and a bathroom, with the little attic up the
ladder. We also have a screened-in back porch as big
as the living room where Mom keeps a lot of stuff in
boxes. This is where we have our famous Lipstick
Wars. No, Tomi, I don't wear lipstick—pew!—do
you? I tried it once but it made me look so phony
and stupid. But my mom, she loves all that Evening
in Paris face powder and Ponds cold cream stuff and
Max Factor Pancake makeup junk. She has lots of
lipsticks in her top drawer she never uses.

So me and Danny, we each borrow one. (Actually
it gets wrecked so we ditch it or throw it out back in
the weeds when we're done.) The redder the better is
our motto. I put on an old shirt and pants and
Danny takes his shirt off, and we stand on opposite
ends of the back porch with our lipsticks drawn. I

yell, On guard! And then we attack each other, duel-
ing with our swords, trying to see who can slash the
most marks. We laugh like crazy. When we hear the
Greyhound bus stop out on the highway, I quick go
up the ladder and change my clothes. Danny hides in
the bathroom and scrubs and puts on his shirt. By the
time Mom comes through the door, I'm putting on
the coffee and getting the potatoes out real fast, ready
to peel. We both are still laughing our heads off!
She's too tired to ask what's so funny.

Other times, when there's nothing else to do, I talk
Danny into playing another game I've invented, and
even though I win every time, it's so exciting he
always plays again. See, we each put on a blindfold
and one of Frankie's old boxing gloves, go to the
opposite ends of the porch, and then come into the
center, swinging. It's scary because you think any
minute you're going to get socked right in the face
and see stars, and sometimes I do, but most of the
time it's Danny that sees stars. He never catches on
that sometimes I slip my blindfold off one eye so I
can see exactly where he is. It's a lot of fun, especially if it's dark and we turn off all the lights. So
when he sees Beverly slug me a good one, his eyes
get all sparkly. But he never cheers her on. We don't

like nobody to pick on nobody in our family. And there's no way Bluto (our new name for Beverly) is ever going to be a member of our family. We're doing fine just the way we are. I don't think Mom really likes Wendall all that much, anyhow. How could she? He's fat and bald and lives in a big old house at a little spot on the side of the highway on the way to Portland. His town doesn't even have a post office. Just a grocery store and a nut house where they dry filberts and walnuts. A good place for Beverly. Wendall has a well-digging business and tells jokes like "It's colder out tonight than a well digger's ass." Which I don't think is funny, do you?

One night when my mom goes for a ride with Wendall, Old Bluto Barf Face starts snooping in our kitchen cupboards. She has her nerve, and I tell her so, and she says, "Nerve nothing. Where's the booze?" I say we don't have any, my mom doesn't drink. She gives me a shove that sends me into the next room and says tell me another one, Blubberbutt. If my dad is hanging around your mom, there's booze in this house, she says. So where is it?

She keeps opening and closing the cupboard doors and pushing stuff aside, but she doesn't find nothing because there's nothing to find. My mom doesn't drink, not since we left my dad, and even then she only drank a little wine once, and I could hear her being sick all night long.

But old Beverly Bluto Boobs stands in the middle of the kitchen with her hands on her hips, snorting like Ferdinand the Bull, you know? Then, Tomi, she's looking at our new garbage can with the copper top, a present from her dad to my mom (how's that for a romantic present?). You know, the kind that has a little pedal that you step on and the lid lifts up? It has a bucket inside, but Mama puts a grocery bag inside so the bucket won't get all gucky with garbage stuff. So here's old Bluto Guts staring at it, and she gets this look in her eye. She pops the top and lifts out the smelly bag of garbage, and guess what? There it is in the bottom of the bucket—a pint of whiskey! Danny says, Hey! Where'd that come from? I can't believe it!

Old Bluto says Good old Dad and grabs the bottle and takes a big slug. Then she digs out a flat silvery bottle from her back pocket and fills it up right to the top. The smell reminds me right away of my daddy, and for a minute I really miss him—him, not that awful whiskey smell.

I'm so surprised at what Blubber Bluto Guts has done that I can't talk. I'm still trying to figure out how come that whiskey got in the garbage in the first place. Now, before Beverly puts it back, she fills the whiskey bottle with water to about where it was before and places it under the sack of garbage again.

So, Tomi, here's old Beverly, sipping from her little bottle, smoking her Lucky Strike right there in our living room. And then, when we hear them pull into the driveway, she flicks the butt out the back door, opens and closes it a couple times fanning the air, and she's all smiles when her dad and my mom come through the front door. And so are they. All smiles, I mean.

The next day, Tomi, my mom tells me Wendall has asked her to marry him. I don't know what to say. I feel awful. She's standing in front of the mirror in the living room looking at herself in her new black dress. It's kind of slinky looking, with this ruffle draped on the hip she calls crepe drape. She's frowning at herself in the mirror, pulling it up on the neck and down on her hips.

She asks me if she looks all right, and I say sure. I wish I could tell her she looks beautiful, but it feels so funny to see her in something so tight like that, I guess I'm embarrassed. She just doesn't look like my mom anymore. Then she wants to know am I really sure, and not to say so if I don't mean it. Her hands are moving up and down, nervous, tugging and pulling at the dress.

I give her a little smile through the mirror and tell her yes, I mean it. I hate to lie like that, Tomi, but she's my mom. Like I said, she needs a lot of encouragement.

She lights a cigarette (she smokes like a chimney!) and turns to look at me, trying hard to catch my eye. She says Maggie, if I marry him, you and Danny will have your own rooms. You'd like that, wouldn't you?

I start to say that the attic is okay, that Danny and me, we're getting used to it, but then she says you'll have to go to another school. So what do you think?

She's waiting for me to say something, but before I can think what to say, she says I won't marry him if you don't want me to. I'll leave it up to you. You decide.

I ask her if Beverly is going to live with us, and she says no, it would be just us, that Beverly would still live with her mother. So what could I say, Tomi? Don't marry him—Danny and me, we hate him? And my mom, with her eyes begging me to say what she wants to hear? So I say Mom, if that's what you want, you should do it.

Just then Wendall's car comes crunching up the gravel driveway. It's him, she says, and takes a last long drag, then pokes the cigarette in the ash box of the stove. She gives me a quick kiss, puts on her coat, and is out the door.

I hurry up the ladder. I'm alone. I lie on my bed staring at the roof boards slanted above my head. I realize now that my dad will never be with us again. I knew it already, but now I know how much I want him to come back to us so that we can be a real family again.

And why do I think that can possibly happen? He's been working in Alaska for over a year and has only written once asking where Frankie is. I wrote him, but I guess I forgot to mail the letter or we were getting ready to move, or something. Now it's too late. My mom has never forgiven Daddy because he has never sent her any money. Every once in a while, she tells me how bad times were with him because of the drinking and all. Other times, when she is mad at me, she tells me I am just like my father. When she talks like that, I always feel like somehow everything is my fault.

That last time when he hit my mama, I told him that I hated him. He got tears in his eyes. I know it hurt him. I felt like crying too, but I didn't. He shouldn't have hit my mama. She's not a kid like Frankie and Danny and me. Mom says that's all water under the bridge now, and over the dam, and not to

cry over spilled milk. She's got all these old sayings
which I think she probably learned from my grandma,
who is pure English but was born in Indiana.

Anyhow, Tomi, before I know what I'm doing,
I'm back down the ladder and fishing out that cigarette butt Mama had stuck in the ashes. I grab some
matches and hurry back up, then strike the match. I
haven't tried smoking since I was a little kid. Guess
what? One puff off that Chesterfield and I'm seeing
spots. I'm so dizzy I have to lie down on my bed. All
my life I've watched my mom smoke, so I just do
what she does, take a big breath and suck it inside.
Wow! When I close my eyes, it feels like the room is
moving round and round, and I'm floating!

But then guess what happens! Someone knocks on
the front door. Tomi, I about jump right out of my
skin! It scares me to death! I'm afraid it might be my
mom coming back for something, so I quick sneak
down the ladder and shove that cigarette back in the
stove. I don't even remember that it can't be my
mom because we never lock our door—she would
just walk in, but I don't have time to think of that
before I hear a man's voice singing, "It's only me
from over the sea,' said Barnacle Bill the Sailor."

I can't believe it—it's my dad! I open the door
and there he stands with his brown Stetson pushed to

the back of his head and this happy look on his face. He has his arms full of packages, which he pushes toward me, and asks do I have a kiss for my old man? I can feel my knees knocking. When he leans down and kisses my cheek, he smells of cigarettes and wet wool, for it is drizzling outside. But he doesn't smell of whiskey! He stands in the middle of the room, looking around.

I ask where'd he come from? He says he just got in from Sitka last night, and didn't I get his letter? I shake my head. Well, mail's bad with the war on, he says, and walks over and peeks into the kitchen. He wants to know where my mom and Danny are. I tell him Danny is at the neighbor's playing dominoes.

When he asks where my mom is, I just say she's out. He frowns at the floor, then wants to know when will she be back. I shrug, then tell him I don't know for sure, that she went to a movie with a friend. I feel my face get hot and can't look right at him because of the lie. He could always tell when us kids were lying by looking into our eyes. But he only smiles a little and asks, aren't I going to invite him to sit down?

So, Tomi, he sits down and I sit down, and then he wants to know where Frankie is, and I tell him about some island whose name I can't remember, and he says Guadalcanal? And I say yeah, that sounds

right. He shakes his head. Then he tells me that today is Pearl Harbor Day, did I remember that it was
a year ago that the Japanese attacked Pearl Harbor
and sank our navy?

I nod yes, and he tells me he's just joined the
army himself today in Portland. I can't believe this,
Tomi. My dad is forty years old! I ask aren't you too
old for any army, and he says no, they are drafting
up to the age of forty-five, so either he signs up now
or he's going to get drafted anyhow. He says he
wants to get overseas and find Frankie. He's worried
about him. He says he wants to be with him so he
can watch out for him. I don't know how he's going
to do that, but I don't ask.

I'm still holding the packages, which he says are
early Christmas presents, because he's leaving tomorrow morning for the army and basic training and
won't be around for Christmas. Which he hasn't been
for a long time before now anyway, but I don't mention that either.

He says the big box is for our mother, a chenille
bed jacket for these cold nights. She always wanted
one of those, he says. I hope she likes it, he says. He
gets a shy look, like he's embarrassed to tell me, but
I can tell he likes what he's done.

He wants to know what time do I think she will

be home because this friend is coming back to pick him up in about half an hour or so—he's got to be back to Portland tonight so he can take the train to Fort Benning, Georgia, first thing in the morning.

I tell him I think it's a double feature, which is another big lie. I have to look at the floor when I say this, then I ask, would he like me to make him some coffee? When he smiles, he covers his mouth, which means he's still missing that front tooth some deputy knocked out the time my mom had the divorce papers served and Frankie and I went to see him in jail. I don't mention the missing tooth. He takes off his hat and rubs his hand across his bald head. If he doesn't smile and show that big black gap in front, he is still handsome, with his dark skin and black eyes and eyebrows. While I make the coffee, I fight back the tears. Here's my dad. Home at last. But not.

I serve him his coffee, black. He sips it boiling hot. I ask how'd he know where to find us, and he says oh, he has his spies.

Just then the back door swings open and Danny is home. He stops cold when he sees our dad, and gets a small grin on his face. Oh, hi, he says, and my dad says for him to come on over and shake his hand, then he asks for a kiss and Danny kisses him on the cheek. My dad points at the present and says, there's

one there for you too, but you can't open it until
Christmas. Then he says what the hell! Go ahead,
and Danny rips the paper off and finds a new pair of
boxing gloves. He looks at me, sees my frown, meaning not to say anything, and he tells Daddy thanks,
it's just what he's always wanted.

So it's my turn, and I open a long shiny blue box
with, guess what? A *pink* comb decorated with
painted *pink* roses and a *pink* brush, a *pink* hand mirror and a little *pink* compact with a little *pink* mirror
and a *pink* lipstick. Tomi, can you believe it? You
know how much I hate *pink*! Danny picks up the
lipstick and laughs out loud, and I tell him to shut
up. My dad looks surprised. You don't talk that way
to your little brother, do you? he asks, and I say
well, maybe sometimes I do, and I laugh a little.

And then, Tomi, we hear the sound of car tires on
the gravel and my dad stands up. He says he guesses
that's his ride. He's gotta leave us kids now. I begin
to shake, not just because I have to say good-bye, but
because I'm not sure that isn't Wendall's car in the
driveway, not Daddy's ride. But then we hear the
horn honk twice, like a signal, and he stands and puts
out his arms and we both go to him and hug and kiss
and say good-bye. We stand at the door and watch
him get into his friend's old Chevy. Before we know

it the car has pulled out, and we see the red taillights shining in the dark, heading toward Portland, which means the car will be passing Wendall's big house somewhere along the highway.

* * *

Later:

Tomi, guess what? I just remembered that I promised my grandma I would never smoke! Why did I do that? I'm so dumb! I broke my promise to my grandma—and I broke my vow to the Girl Reserves too! Oh, I wish you were here, Tomi.

January 31, 1943

Dear Tomi,

Please excuse me for not mailing these letters, but I'm still waiting, hoping you will write again so I will have your new address. Where are you? It's been almost six months since I heard from you. Please, please write to me soon. I'm going to keep writing to you, Tomi, because when I do, I feel like you are almost here and we are just talking the way we used to. Except I'm telling you things I would be too shy to say to your face. I think that's what's so good about writing.

So now, my mom's going to marry Wendall next Saturday. Which just goes to prove who the really crazy one is—me! If I hadn't told her to go ahead and marry him, she probably wouldn't have said yes, and Danny and I wouldn't have to move. This time we start all over again in a different town. So of course we'll be going to another school. She says we'll be moving in two or three weeks. And guess who gets to have a big stepsister? I don't want to think about it, any of it.

***

Later:

Oh, gee, I have to tell you one more thing that happened Saturday, but you've got to *promise promise promise* you won't tell a single soul. It's a secret, Tomi! Buddy kissed me! And I liked it! So I kissed him back! Here's what happened. All of a sudden, he shows up in Jacob's old Essex and parks in our drive-way. I'm so surprised I don't know how to act. He's hardly said a word to me at school, and he sits right behind me in Latin class. He came to tell me he just got his driver's license and that Mr. Johnson recommended him for that job at the Thoroughbred farm after all! He'll get to train to be a real jockey, but first he'll just be exercising and feeding the horses and stuff. He's so happy, and so am I. He seems just like his old self, and wants to know, do I want to take a ride out to Mr. Johnson's pasture to visit poor old Bob? We take the back road.

It's drizzling and kind of cold in that old car, so we're just sitting there inside looking out at poor old Bob when, all of a sudden, Buddy leans over and kisses me right on the mouth! And like I said, I do the same. And Tomi, I just want to stay there forever—I don't want it ever to stop! But after about twenty minutes I get scared of what Buddy is doing with his hands. I push them away so he can't touch my boobs, then he gets real close and pushes up against me, and, oh, Tomi! all of a sudden I remember what my mom said about how easy it is for a girl to get pregnant. Then I really get scared! So I make Buddy stop. Oh, boy, when we do, we can't see out the windows—they're all fogged up. Then Buddy tells me he will drive all the back roads and come to see me in our new place, and he gives me his Hi-Y pin to wear. We're going steady!!! I'm so happy!!! *Tomi, I'm in love!!!*

February 15, 1943

Dear Tomi,

I feel terrible to have to tell you this, but when my mom found out that I have been writing to you all this time, she got real mad because she says that people say the police found a shortwave radio in your vegetable stand last year, and that your daddy is a spy. She says I'm being real unpatriotic and disloyal to Frankie, who is in the South Pacific fighting the war. She says he could be killed any minute, don't I even care? I said of course I care about my brother. I don't want him to be hurt, but I also care about you, my friend, and that I don't believe that about your father. Besides, you are an American citizen just like us, and your two brothers joined the army just like Frankie, they are soldiers just like he is. I told her it wasn't right to make your whole family go live in that cow stall and then send you away to some camp. I started to cry, but she just looked real mad and said, *That's enough, Maggie! You are not writing any more letters.*

Lost and Found

My Latin teacher, Miss Tennessee Weathered, is as tall as a hollyhock and almost as slender. At least, that's how she seems that first day of school when she stands before us cradling the small Latin book in her two hands as if it were a baby bird fallen from a nest. Her skin beneath the fine layer of pinkish face powder appears to be as papery thin as a petal of the hollyhock flower itself. She makes me think of the hollyhock that sways gently beside the sink window in my grandma's kitchen. Virginia says I like to exaggerate everything, and that her skin is just wrinkled and old, and without all that powder she would look like a dried-up old prune, and that she looks more like Olive Oyl than a hollyhock. Actually, Virginia is right. I do like to exaggerate sometimes. Except that Miss Weathered never sways in any breeze. Her back is as straight as a broom handle. I don't know how tall she is but from my seat in front I have to tip my head back to look up at her like I do when I'm sitting in the first row of the Ritz Theater. Her breath smells like peppermints.

Each day she wears a straight black dress with either white lace or a small white collar, sometimes with a fat red velvet rose pinned at the neck, and her hair is very black. Virginia says that's because she dyes it, but if she does, I can't tell. She looks very strict, until she smiles. Then she looks like the pink of her skin is coming from deep inside, like the glow in the sky at a summer's sunset. Virginia says she's an old maid who's never been married or had any kids. Virginia is critical because she's having a lot of trouble keeping her *puer*s and *puella*s straight, and blames it on Miss Weathered, who I think is a very good teacher.

When school first started last fall, and I told my mom I had her for my Latin class, my mom said, "Good Lord, is she still there? She was my botany teacher when I was a girl! We thought she was ancient then. I wonder if she remembers me?"

I don't know and I don't ask. I'm kind of shy around Miss Weathered. She's the advisor for the Girl Reserves, and also for the school yearbook, the *Annual*. When she learned I like to draw cartoons, she put me in charge of making the posters for the club meetings, and asked me if I would like to submit some cartoons for the yearbook.

I said yes. So that's how I've become a school cartoonist, doing posters for other clubs besides the Girl Reserves. I'm now busy drawing one hundred and fifty tickets for the big Pep Club football dance coming up this Friday night. I'm not worried. I'll finish them tonight. Each ticket is a cartoon figure of a football player wearing a helmet and holding a football, which I draw on poster board and cut out with scissors. I'm very careful not to smear the India ink when I ink in the details, and set each one aside to dry. It makes me think of that time when Aunt Ramona-Ramona let me finish painting Maggie and Jiggs, and I knew for sure right that minute that I was going to be an artist when I grew up. I still have that painting in my treasure box. When I look at it now, I remember lots of things that happened when I was just a kid. I especially remember Aunt Ramona-Ramona, who I pretend is still my aunt.

After I rinse the Speedball pen point in a glass of water, I sit back to admire my work. Already I have fifty-four small tickets, and it's only Saturday morning. I'll have the hundred and fifty tickets to take to school on Monday easy.

I won't be going to the dance. We'll be packing our

things next Friday night. Saturday we'll be moving to Wendall's house. A new town, a new school, a new stepfather, a new stepsister, a new last name for my mother. Ebersole. Frankie and Danny and I, our last name will always be Morrison. What will the teachers and the kids think when they find out I have a different name from my mom's?

Buddy wants me to go with him to the dance now that I am wearing his Hi-Y pin and we are going steady. He says he will come and get me in Jacob's old Essex, and take me home. Mom says okay, I can go if I get all my packing done and help Danny do his. Also to throw away as much as I can of both our things because we are getting a fresh start and don't want to clutter up Wendall's house with old junk. So now I just have to figure out what I'm going to wear, which won't be hard because it's only supposed to be school clothes.

My mom and Wendall got married last Saturday by a justice of the peace in Portland. They spent a night at the Benson Hotel—which is supposed to be very fancy—but she says she's much too tired to act like a brand-new bride. Wendall is coming on Saturday with a truck to move us to his house, with its five bedrooms and a big garden, but she has to work each day this week and do the packing at night. I tell her I thought when you got married you got to stay home and take care of the house for your husband. But she says it's different the second time around, especially when you have three half-grown kids. Even though Frankie is overseas and won't be living with us, he still counts, she says.

I've been going through all my stuff, sorting out what to take and throwing away the rest. Mostly it's old drawings on pieces of cardboard my mom brings home from the store, the stiff white paper that separates each pair of hose in the boxes of silk stockings she sorts and prices at the store. Part of me wants to keep everything so I can share it with my children someday. I want them to know what I was like when I was their ages, but I'm burning all the drawings in the stove, except for one, my comic strip I call William Tell, and the Maggie and Jiggs drawing I just mentioned. I'm keeping the white clay coiled pot I painted turquoise blue, which I made in sixth grade. The white clay felt like having my hands in Nucoa or Crisco. The first coil is cracked because it didn't get baked. I keep all my report cards since first grade with red and gold stars; the book *Little Women* I won for reading the most library books in my age group the summer I was eleven; my dark green glass Japanese float and little Goofy dolls; my Tillie the Toiler and Betty Boop paper dolls I cut out of the newspaper before Daddy lost his job on the jetty in

Newport; my Palmer Method penmanship award from Waldport school, where I got to use a real pen and ink—before they kicked me out and made me go to the camp one-room schoolhouse; my Brownie camera, which I earned the money for by selling hand-painted Easter eggs at the entrance to Ziegler's market; and the little scrapbook my mom gave me for my small photos of Tomi, Donny, Fritzie, and Buddy, who appear so small you can hardly see who they are, the sun so bright their eyes are black holes in their faces. But I know who they are.

When I get to the letters I wrote to Tomi, I sit back and think: my mom has forbidden me to write to Tomi anymore, but she didn't say I couldn't send the letters I've already written. Before I move I've got to find out where Tomi is. What camp did the government send her to after she and her family left that cow stall in Portland? Would Miss Weathered know?

✳ ✳ ✳

Monday, on my way to math class, I see Miss Weathered standing in front of her open classroom door.

"Oh, Maggie!" she says. "I was just thinking of you."

"You were?"

"Yes, dear, I have some good news for you. I was

wondering if you could see me after lunch, before we start our Latin class?"

"Okay, sure. I wanted to ask you something too."

Just then the first bell rings. "Oh, dear, I'm sorry, but can it wait until we meet later?"

"Okay." I turn and bump into Virginia, who gives me a friendly shove back with her shoulder so that I almost drop my books. Virginia herself is not carrying a single book, since she doesn't believe in studying. She doesn't plan to go to college because she is taking lessons to become a roller-skating champion. She spends her evenings and weekends at the skating rink practicing special tricks in the center of the ring, like being spun by Harold while she hooks her shoe skates up on his arms, lets go with her hands, and drops her body so that she is flying around in a circle, pageboy hairdo flying straight out like the wind sock at the airport in a high wind. I tried it with Harold once but could only get my two skates hooked on his arms, which about killed me. My body sagged and Harold could hardly get us twirling in a circle. When we stopped I later discovered I had a split in the seat of my shorts. I was too embarrassed to try it again. Besides, Harold said I wasn't the type. Actually, he said I was a real chunk. Virginia is taller than I am. She's skinny everywhere but in the top, where she makes up for the rest of her.

Since Tomi left, Virginia and I eat lunch together in the cafeteria. I eat my baloney sandwiches and listen to her go on and on about Harold this and Harold that. Later, in the girls' bathroom, she tells me Harold thinks she's ready for the state championship competition this summer in Salem. She's standing in front of the mirror in the girls' bathroom putting on her Tangee—Flame Glow—lipstick. "I'm going to have a special skating outfit made with spangles and satin, and my own shoe skates—white, I think, but maybe dyed the same color as my outfit. What do you think?"

I don't see how she can put on lipstick and still keep talking, but she does. "Sounds real good, I guess."

"I haven't decided what color yet. Harold says he'll take me to this special place in Portland where you buy theatrical costumes and stuff. He has his own car and lots of gasoline, and he doesn't worry about gas rationing, but don't ask me where he gets it."

Which I know means he's siphoning gas with a rubber hose out of gas tanks. "Aren't you afraid he'll get arrested?"

Virginia laughs. "They'll have to catch him first. He knows what he's doing."

"Oh?" I watch her fooling around with her lipstick, which looks orange in the tiny tube but turns her lips pink. I think of Danny and our famous Lipstick Wars.

She gives me the shoulder bump again. "Hey, what's the matter with you? You're awful quiet today. Break up with your boyfriend?" I've told Virginia I'm going steady with Buddy, but I haven't worn his Hi-Y pin to school yet. My mom tells me I am too young to go steady, and besides, we're moving, so don't be silly. It's just puppy love anyhow, she says, and that won't last, so don't get carried away with all that. You haven't finished packing up all your stuff, so get to it! "Just trying to decide what to wear to the dance, is all," I say.

Lots of times I hear my mom's voice when she isn't around, almost as if she's standing right there in front of me—or in some special place in my head, like sitting on a wooden stool right behind my left eyebrow. About the only time I feel like I am really alone to be myself is when I'm drawing or trying to write a poem—which I'm not any good at and which isn't very often these days anyway.

I watch Virginia kiss a piece of toilet paper and admire her perfect pink Tangee lips; then I ask, "Do you know where Tomi was sent?"

"Tomi? You mean Tomi Katayama? No, why do you want to know that?"

"I want to send her a letter." I try to avoid looking at myself in the mirror. I don't want to see how frizzy my hair is even after two months, ever since my mother insisted that I get a permanent wave from Wendall's sister Jewel, who owns the beauty shop above the Rexall drugstore.

One Saturday morning, Jewel sat me in front of the mirror so I could watch her hook me up to her electric permanent wave machine. With much combing of sloppy smelly stuff into my hair and wrapping with slippery paper, she rolled and clamped each one to a small metal curler attached to fifty thick wires that hung from the big machine.

At the age of fourteen and a half, I was being beautified through electrocution by order of my mother, and for what good reason? Because she wanted to get that "damn cowlick trained so that you don't go through life looking like Skeezix." Without my cowlick I don't even look like myself, and I'm too old to look like Shirley Temple. In fact, if I were a redhead, I'd look like Little Orphan Annie, without her dog, Sandy.

I wanted to barf and cry when Jewel finally unplugged me from that machine and combed my hairdo with thick gooey stuff to make it look like Grandma's, whose thin white hair Jewel also does sometimes. The frizz I have now is partly because I'd run and walked the two miles home so that I could douse my head under the kitchen faucet to wash the stink of ammonia and tight sausage curls out of my hair. When my mother came home from work that night, she had a fit. She said I'd ruined a perfectly good permanent (which she got at a discount because she was going to marry Jewel's brother). That made me smile, but not so she could see me. And she finally got her way. I have to wear a bow ribbon in my hair all the time now to hold the frizz out of my eyes.

"Want to use my lipstick?" Virginia asks.

"No, thanks." Oh, swell, that's all I need to make the picture perfect. My frizz and Tangee lips. Buddy would really want to kiss me then.

"No kidding, you'd look a lot better." She makes as if to put some on my lips. I push her hand away, harder than I mean to, and the tip of the soft lipstick hits the mirror and is smashed.

"Well, thanks a lot, Maggie Morrison! Look what you done now, dammit, you've ruined it! That cost me a whole twenty cents! I give up on you, you're such a moron! When are you going to act your age and grow up? You can't be some dumb tomboy all your life. You should at least try to look like a girl, not be so plain all the time. Really, I honestly don't get what Buddy sees in you!" She heads for the door, then turns. "Come to think of it, he's not so hot himself. He's just as big a moron as you are. He probably hasn't even kissed you, let alone done anything else like Harold and me. So grow up, why don't you!" She stomps toward the door, then turns. "And don't think I'm going to forget this."

"Virginia, I'm sorry." But the bathroom door slams shut. I'm alone. I look at myself in the mirror. Virginia is right. I do look like a moron. I am plain. I'm surprised I never noticed it before. I guess I never really looked at myself, that is, really looked at myself. But now I see it for the first time. I'm ugly! *I'm ugly, ugly, ugly!* My hair is mousy brown, my face is too fat—in fact, *I am fat.* My eyes are too dark, my eyebrows too black, too thick, my teeth are too big, my dimples look stupid in my fat cheeks, I'm getting a big pimple right in the middle of my forehead. So what does Buddy see in me? He must be blind. What's wrong with him anyhow?

I jump when I hear the first bell for fifth period. I was supposed to see Miss Weathered before my Latin class! I grab up my books and run down the hall. She is standing by her door. Some kids are already going into the classroom. Buddy cuts his eyes at me and gives me a shy smile. I look down at my shoes, too ugly to smile back. He must be a first-class moron if he really likes me.

"Maggie, I only have a minute, dear, so let's talk right after this period, all right? And you say you have a question you want to ask me?"

I can't speak, but I nod and go to my seat. Buddy smiles again but I look out the window, although I see Virginia well enough. She's glaring at me, still mad. I don't care. I never liked her anyhow. She's cheap and fast and tough, and she can have her big Harold and state's skating championship. He's probably a sex fiend. She'll learn the hard way. The only reason we hang around together is because Tomi isn't here anymore.

When the class bell rings, I wait as Miss Weathered opens the door and says "See you tomorrow" as everyone but me leaves for the next class. My next class is study hall. Miss Weathered asks me to stay seated and sits down at the desk beside me.

"Don't worry, Maggie, I'll write you an excuse. I don't have a class this period so we can talk. Is that all right?"

"Yes, okay." I don't know what to expect, so I'm a little nervous, waiting. Then she smiles.

"Well, you know, we are so pleased with the wonderful artwork you are doing for the Girl Reserves and also for some of the other clubs, that the Girl Reserves board has chosen you to be our publicity chairman. That is, if you would like that. You would be a member of the board, of course. And there would not be any real change in the work you will be doing, since you already are doing such a good job. It's just that we would like to honor you for being so willing to use your talent to serve in your own way, you see? It's very unusual to choose a freshman to be on the board. It's usually a position held by a junior or senior, but with your enthusiasm and willingness to work so hard, we thought, well, you've earned it, so why wait?" She pauses and smiles that lovely pink sunset smile, then asks, "So what do you think about this? Do you want to think it over for a day or two?"

I shake my head. I can't speak. I swallow, but the lump in my throat won't go away. I feel my eyes getting watery and look down at my shoes again. I'm so proud I could burst. And so sad at the same time.

"My dear, what is it?"

"Miss Weathered, my mom got married last weekend. We're moving this Saturday. I won't be going to school here anymore."

"Oh, my dear! What a surprise!" She sounds flustered and upset. I look up and see that the sun has left her cheeks. Her face looks very tired and is covered with tiny wrinkles. "Of course, I'm happy for your mother, dear. I had her in my botany class years ago, a lovely girl, your mother, but not the student you are. Oh, I shouldn't say that, I know, but I've enjoyed having you in my class so very much." She removes a white embroidered handkerchief pinned to her shoulder like a corsage and gently wipes my eyes, then dabs at her own. "Well," she says, "I'd better write you a pass to study hall. We'll talk some more, Maggie dear. Come see me again this week and we'll talk about your future at your new school, will you do that?"

I nod and pick up my books as she writes me a pass. Before I open the door to leave, she calls, "Maggie, didn't you say you had a question you wanted to ask me?"

"Uh-huh. Do you happen to know Tomi Katayama's address?"

"Tomi? Why, yes, I do! I have it right here." Miss Weathered opens her desk drawer. "I just got a nice long letter from her yesterday. Here, let me copy the address out for you."

ABOUT THE AUTHOR

MOLLIE POUPENEY, a nationally recognized
ceramic artist, has exhibited her distinctive coil-
built burnished and painted pottery in the United
States and in other parts of the world. A native
of Oregon, she is a graduate of Providence
School of Nursing, Portland, and the University
of California, Berkeley. She is married and the
mother of two daughters and one son. She lives
with her husband, Leon, in Moraga, California,
and in Ashland, Oregon. *Her Father's Daughter* is
her first novel.

HER FATHER'S DAUGHTER

by Mollie Poupeney

A READERS GUIDE

Questions for Discussion

1. Discuss the meaning of the title. Maggie's father is largely absent from her life. Even when he's present, he offers her little emotional support. And through most of the novel, he does not live with the family. Why did Mollie Poupeney name the novel *Her Father's Daughter*? What is it about Maggie that makes her "her father's daughter"?

2. The novel is told in a series of episodes in Maggie's life, with the link being either the presence or absence of her father. Between the chapters "Daddy for Sale" and "Big Boy Now," there is a gap of almost two years. Fill in that gap. Imagine what might have transpired.

3. Maggie knows that she has no say in what happens to her. "Like somebody else gets to be the boss of my life all the time." (p. 139) How is this true for most kids?

4. Maggie's relationship with men in the novel is problematic. While she loves her father and is very much like him, he is an alcoholic, abusive, and neglectful. Her mother's boss and Uncle Lester abuse her. How might this affect her relationships later in life?

5. Throughout the story, Maggie is allowed to go just about anywhere she wants by herself. Do you see this as parental neglect or just the nature of the time and place? How does it compare with the way things are now?

6. *Her Father's Daughter* spans seven years of Maggie's life. How does she change from the beginning of the novel to the end?

7. The author's descriptions of even the secondary characters in the novel—Goofy John, Aunt Fern, Aunt Ramona, Uncle Lester, Buddy, Buddy's grandma, and Beverly— are so clear you can easily see them in your mind's eye. Which characters would you like to invite to your book group or to your house for dinner? Why?

8. "First, I decide I will begin with very small bites. But all of a sudden, there goes the whole thing right in my mouth. One bite, and all this sweet cherry juice is squirting on my tongue and filling the back of my throat! . . . I want it to last forever." (pp. 29–30) Pick a favorite candy or food and describe eating it in the same way that Maggie describes eating those two chocolate-covered cherries.

9. *Her Father's Daughter* is filled with figures of speech— such as "take a long walk off a short pier," "spit in the wind," "six shingles short of a shed roof," and "see a man about a horse"—that were commonly used in the logging towns of the Pacific Northwest during the 1930s. Talk about what each expression means.

10. Maggie's school friend Tomi Katayama and her family are interned in a camp, as were thousands of Japanese Americans during World War II. What does this say about the mood of the country during the war? Is this something that could happen again to another group of people given the present state of affairs?

11. The Depression was "hard times" for most people living in America, but it was even more so for Maggie and her family. Why was life so hard for them? What is the turning point in the novel when things seem to get a little better?

This guide was prepared by Clifford Wohl, educational consultant.

In Her Own Words

A CONVERSATION
with
MOLLIE POUPENEY

Q. In the acknowledgments, you thank the authors of the comic strips of the thirties and forties. And your novel begins with a warm family scene centered on the Sunday funnies. Maggie herself draws cartoons. What were some of the comics and the comic-strip characters you grew up with, and why they are so important to you?

A. The funny papers—which we now call the comics—are a unique American popular art. They flourished in the Depression thirties and wartime forties. The funny papers provided a way to learn to draw, by copying favorite characters—Tillie the Toiler, Betty Boop, Tarzan of the Apes, Katrinka on the Toonerville Trolley, the Katzenjammer Kids, Maggie and Jiggs, Little Orphan Annie (who never got her eyeballs). I had my own comic strip in the sixties and seventies called *Out to Lunch*, which ran in some college papers in the U.S.—and in a school in Thessaloníki, Greece. I still work on my cartoons, translating them into color on my computer. Great fun!

Q. Since this is your first published novel, we'd like to ask you several questions about the writing process to encourage your young readers who are also aspiring writers. When did you first think you could be an author?

A. It never occurred to me that I could be an author. Occasionally, I did write poetry, which I rarely shared. Then, when certain painful childhood memories kept pushing at me, I recognized they might make stories and tried to write some of them. I took a few writing classes and in this way began to share stories with other aspiring writers. From one class, we formed a writers' group. I wrote three unsuccessful novels before I wrote the stories for *Daughter*.

Q. How did you discipline yourself to work on your novel? Did you set specific goals in terms of number of pages or number of hours?

A. Most of the time, I felt more compelled than disciplined. A story would begin to grow in my mind and demanded my attention. If I got the first line, then I could begin to write. I never set specific goals other than to make the story better if I could. Sometimes, I just wrote until I ran out of words. Sometimes, when the subject was getting too close to my own childhood pain, I would be blocked for a while and would be depressed. After a time, I could take it up again and get it out—the thing that had caused me the painful memory. I needed to find the truth in the experience. Some of my experiences had never been shared before I wrote them down.

Q. How long did _Her Father's Daughter_ take to write? How long did it take to get published?

A. Some of the stories in _Her Father's Daughter_ took years. For one thing, it took that long to learn to write well enough, find the right voice, the point of view, and the tone, the motivation, and the feelings of the characters. But I was also teaching and working in clay for most of that time.

Q. You mentioned two writing groups among your acknowledgments. What role did they play—beyond support and encouragement—in shaping your novel?

A. I received plenty of helpful criticism along the way, most of which I acted upon. But one thing that was very helpful to me was the practice of reading my work aloud to a group and hearing for myself how the words sounded when read aloud—the rhythm of the sentences. Sometimes I could tell just by reading where something was off. The other thing was the gratifying feeling of having a responsive audience to read to whose reactions told you what impact the story had. If someone laughs in the right place, that's just a great thing! Also, it gives you a great opportunity to ham it up a bit, become your own actor in the story. I've become a great fan of books on tape for that reason—the reader becomes the actor of all parts.

Q. Many first novels are autobiographical. Is this true for you?

A. All of my writing has been autobiographical, fictionalized, often with a twist. For example, in [the chapter] "Goofy John," there was such a person who made little seashell dolls and also a woman who had the candy store with the chocolate-covered cherries. The setting was accurate; the family was my own. My mother baked bread and took in laundry, there was a dead whale on the beach, and my father did drink on Saturday nights. But he didn't blow up the dead whale and Goofy John didn't die that way. Also there was no Raynaldo, the old Chihuahua. And I never got to have a chocolate-covered cherry. So I gave myself not one, but two!

Q. What kind of research did you do for the historical aspects of the novel and its setting?

A. I interviewed old loggers who knew my father and told me how the hard times were for them; read old newspapers at the University of Oregon; visited the Douglas County logging museum. But mostly, I dug deeper into my own memories for the sights and smells and sounds of a family living close.

Q. You are a nationally recognized ceramic artist. What is the same about writing a novel and creating a piece of pottery? What is different?

A. I wouldn't say I was a *nationally* recognized ceramic artist these days. I haven't exhibited or worked in clay for over ten years, not since I had ovarian cancer. Clay work takes a lot of muscle. Luckily, writing takes a different kind of muscle—the one between the ears—so writing then became my primary focus. I began to concentrate fully on it for the first time. Writing and working in clay are like two fingers on the same hand—both important, each part of the creative process. And the ability to become completely immersed in your art is something that must be brought to your work, no matter what work you do.

Q. If *Her Father's Daughter* were a piece of pottery, what would it look like?

A. You'd have to see my pottery to understand, but I'll try to explain. My pottery is hand-built by coils. Many of the pots are big. The surface is smoothed and polished with a shiny polishing quartz stone, the way the Indians do their pottery. No glaze. After it has been fired, I take a small hammer and break the pot into many pieces. I then fire each piece individually in the fireplace and glue the pieces together like a jigsaw puzzle. When the pot is reconstructed, it shows the random fire patterns and changes. It has been transformed. Sometimes I drill small holes and lace parts of the pot together; sometimes I hang a pendant of different colors and kinds of beads from the lacing. This I call the Tail of the Pot.

It's possible to see pottery as a metaphor for writing, or for life itself. If *Her Father's Daughter* were a piece of my pottery, each story would be one shard with a separate and individual shape, but an inherent part of the structure that shapes the whole, thus making the book.

Q. Your novel is structured as distinct episodic chapters as opposed to following a single story line. Does this reflect your view of life or is it the way Maggie perceives her life?

A. I conceived *Her Father's Daughter* not as a novel but as a group of related stories about one family as told from the point of view of Maggie Morrison. As I mentioned, I had already written three novels—one about the Morrison family—with pretty much the same stories. I deliberately chose the short story format because I felt it was the best way to show how a child's life is affected by parents, family situations, other adults. In other words, life itself.

Q. Most of the novel is told in first-person narrative, but several chapters are in the third person. What effect were you trying to create by changing the voice?

A. Maggie is the protagonist, yes. Most of the stories are told in her voice and in the present tense. The first story, "The Tale of the Frog," is actually told from both Maggie's and her little brother Danny's points of view. The other two exceptions are the ones told from the point of view of Danny, in the third person. I did this because these stories—"Big Boy Now" and "Milk Toast for Supper"— revealed something about Maggie that couldn't be told as well in her own voice. I felt it was more powerful to tell it through the eyes of the more innocent five-year-old boy. The story "Mr. Johnson's Pasture" is the only one told from Maggie's point of view in the third person. This was an oversight. I originally wrote all my stories in the past tense. When I converted them to the present tense, I actually forgot to do that one.

Q. In young adult novels, for good or for bad, the main character usually has some impact on the direction and resolution of the story. This is not true for Maggie. Is that because Maggie is a victim, or is it that children really have no control over their lives?

A. What kind of control does any child have over his or her life? Every day millions of children are emotionally and physically battered, molested, and harassed at home and in school. Many never feel that they are loved by anyone and may never learn how to love themselves or another person. The situation where Maggie is molested by her mother's boss is autobiographical. It's a common kind of offense that young girls experience, one they may never tell a soul about, that can mark them for life. How can there be a happy ending to Maggie's story when her life is so uncertain? You ask if Maggie is a victim. If she is, she doesn't know it. But by drawing on her own resources, she is definitely a survivor. For me, that is the impact of the story.

Oregon Blue Book

A state history of the Great Depression.

www.bluebook.state.or.us/cultural/history/history25.htm

Franklin D. Roosevelt Library & Digital Archives

A description of the Depression and of President Roosevelt's program called the New Deal.

www.fdrlibrary.marist.edu/depress.html

American Council on Alcoholism

Information from a nonprofit organization that educates the public about the dangers of alcohol.

www.aca-usa.org

Coconino County

Historical information on the early-twentieth-century cartoon *Krazy Kat* and related characters.

www.krazy.com/biblio.htm

H. H. Knerr

How *The Katzenjammer Kids* comics were drawn by H. H. Knerr.

www.geocities.com/~jimlowe/knerr/knerrdex.html

Bud, Not Buddy
CHRISTOPHER PAUL CURTIS
0-440-41328-1

In this Newbery Award Winner, Bud's search for
his father brings adventure during a trip through
Depression-era Michigan.

A Part of the Sky
ROBERT NEWTON PECK
0-679-88696-6

Times are difficult during the Great Depression, and
thirteen-year-old Rob Peck must struggle to keep his
family together after the death of his father.

A Door Near Here
HEATHER QUARLES
0-440-22761-5

Because of her mother's struggle with alcoholism,
fifteen-year-old Katherine must take care of her family.

I Hadn't Meant to Tell You This
JACQUELINE WOODSON
0-440-21960-4

Lena has a terrifying secret. Can her new friend
Marie help? Or will Marie make things worse?

Kit's Wilderness
DAVID ALMOND
0-440-41605-1
Kit Watson and John Askew look for the childhood
ghosts of their long-gone ancestors in the mines
of Stoneygate.

Skellig
DAVID ALMOND
0-440-22908-1
Michael feels helpless because of his baby sister's
illness, until he meets a creature called Skellig.

Heaven Eyes
DAVID ALMOND
0-440-22910-3
Erin Law and her friends in the orphanage are
labeled Damaged Children. They run away one night,
traveling downriver on a raft. What they find on their
journey is stranger than you can imagine.
Available October 2002

Becoming Mary Mehan: Two Novels
JENNIFER ARMSTRONG
0-440-22961-8
Set against the events of the American Civil War,
The Dreams of Mairhe Mehan depicts an Irish
immigrant girl and her family, who are struggling to
find their place in the war-torn country. *Mary Mehan
Awake* takes up Mary's story after the war, when she
must begin a journey of renewal.

Forgotten Fire
ADAM BAGDASARIAN
0-440-22917-0

In 1915, Vahan Kenderian is living a life of privilege when
his world is shattered by the Turkish-Armenian War.

Ghost Boy
IAIN LAWRENCE
0-440-41668-X

Fourteen-year-old Harold Kline is an albino—an outcast. When
the circus comes to town, Harold runs off to join it in hopes of
discovering who he is and what he wants in life. Is he a circus
freak or just a normal guy?

Gathering Blue
LOIS LOWRY
0-440-22949-9

Lamed and suddenly orphaned, Kira is mysteriously removed
to live in the palatial Council Edifice, where she is expected
to use her gifts as a weaver to do the bidding of the
all-powerful Guardians.
Available September 2002

The Giver
LOIS LOWRY
0-440-23768-8

Jonas's world is perfect. Everything is under control. There is
no war or fear or pain. There are no choices, until Jonas is
given an opportunity that will change his world forever.
Available September 2002

Both Sides Now
RUTH PENNEBAKER
0-440-22933-2

A compelling look at breast cancer through the eyes of a
mother and daughter. Liza must learn a few life lessons from
her mother, Rebecca, about the power of family.
Available July 2002

Her Father's Daughter
MOLLIE POUPENEY
0-440-22879-4
As she matures from a feisty tomboy of seven to a
spirited young woman of fourteen, Maggie discovers
that the only constant in her life of endless new
homes and new faces is her ever-emerging
sense of herself.

The Baboon King
ANTON QUINTANA
0-440-22907-3
Neither Morengáru's father's Masai tribe nor his
mother's Kikuyu tribe accepts him. Banished from
both tribes, Morengáru encounters a baboon troop
and faces a fight with the simian king.

Holes
LOUIS SACHAR
0-440-22859-X
Stanley has been unjustly sent to a boys'
detention center, Camp Green Lake. But there's
more than character improvement going on at the
camp—the warden is looking for something.

Memories of Summer
RUTH WHITE
0-440-22921-9
In 1955, thirteen-year-old Lyric describes her older
sister Summer's descent into mental illness, telling
Summer's story with humor, courage, and love.